Peter Dickinson's
The Kin

PO'S STORY

D1409028

Peter Dickinson's
The Kin

PO'S STORY

GROSSET & DUNLAP • NEW YORK

Copyright © 1998 by Peter Dickinson.
Cover art copyright © 1998 by Nenad Jakesevic. All rights reserved.
Published by Grosset & Dunlap, Inc.,
a member of Penguin Putnam Books for Young Readers, New York.
GROSSET & DUNLAP is a trademark of Grosset & Dunlap, Inc.
Published simultaneously in Canada.
Printed in the U.S.A.

Library of Congress Cataloging-in-Publication Data
Dickinson, Peter, 1927-
Po's story.
p.   cm — (Peter Dickinson's The Kin)
Summary: As a member of the Kin, a band of people living
in prehistoric times, young Po wants to prove his bravery
but finds that doing so requires overcoming great obstacles.
[1. Prehistoric peoples—Fiction. 2. Survival—Fiction.]
I. Title. II. Series: Dickinson, Peter, 1927-   Peter Dickinson's The Kin.
PZ7.D562Po 1998 [Fic]—dc21 98-33908 CIP AC

ISBN 0-448-41711-1
A B C D E F G H I J

For Sam and Andrew

Peter Dickinson's

The Kin

PO'S STORY

Before you start...

About two hundred thousand years ago, on a hot continent, the first true, modern human beings evolved. There were other humans before them, but these were our direct ancestors.

The real people who lived then left very few traces—the stone tools they made, some fossils of their own bones and the bones of animals they ate, the ashes of their fires, and so on. What were they like? How did they live? Even the experts can only guess, using their imaginations and the few facts they do know. So that's what I've done too in my stories about the Kin. I've made almost everything up.

This book is about a boy called Po. He belongs to the Moonhawk Kin. They and the seven other Kins used to live in what they now call the old Good Places, but five years ago they were attacked and driven out by a horde of murderous strangers. Only half the Moonhawks, with a few people from other Kins, survived. After various adventures (which you can read about in *Suth's Story* and *Noli's Story*), they reached the New Good Places and settled down there. Now though, they are being forced to move on, and face new dangers.

Some experts believe that one of the things that made these people different from earlier humans was that they had language. They could speak. This meant they could tell stories. They told stories to help make sense of their world, to explain anything from who made it to why a particular rock is called by its name. Then they began to tell stories for the sheer pleasure of storytelling.

So, between the chapters of these books, I've put what the Kin call Oldtales to show what some of their stories might have been like.

—Peter Dickinson

1

No rains came.

For moon after moon after moon the sky stayed the same harsh blue. All day the sun glared down. The nights were very cold, but no dew formed.

The grasses withered, with empty seed heads. The roots that people could eat shriveled in the ground. If nuts formed, they were empty shells.

The river dwindled to a stream, to a trickle, to a few stinking pools. When they were gone, it ran underground, and then the people had to dig down till they reached the water and scooped it out handful by handful.

When they did this, animals smelled the water from far away and came for it, desperate to drink, but weak with hunger and thirst. This made them easy to hunt, but there was not much meat on them.

And people were not the only hunters. There were lions and cheetahs and packs of wild dogs and hyenas. They too smelled the water and came to it, knowing that they would find both drink and food. People might be food, if they didn't set lookouts. Lookout was something a half-grown child could do. Even Po, though he'd had to ask.

Po had climbed a tree. It was dead, because of the drought, so there were no leaves to screen his view. It was a bit far from the water hole, so he'd really need to shout if danger threatened.

He was pleased with himself. When the men had been arranging their hunt he had nudged Suth and whispered, "Suth, I do lookout? I, Po, ask." Suth had smiled and spoken to Tun, who was leader, and Tun had glanced at Po and nodded. So Po was one of the two lookouts. Nar was the other, over on the far side of the dry riverbed. Nar was Po's private enemy.

"Keep good watch, Po," Suth had told him quietly. "Do not dream."

But of course Po dreamed. He was always full of dreams. This time he was the hero of the hunt. Antelope would come to the water and the hunters would spring their ambush, but they'd be unlucky. Someone— Net, probably—would move too soon and the antelope would take fright and race away across the plain. The best of them—a glossy great buck—he must have found good grass somewhere to have all that meat on him—would run close by Po's tree, and clever Po had taken a couple of good rocks up with him, and now he slung one at the buck, slung it with deadly aim, catching him full force on the side of the head, just in the right spot below the ear, and…and…

Po hadn't decided on the end of the dream. Would he kill the buck outright? That seemed a bit much, even for a dream. Perhaps he'd just stun it, so that it lost its bearings and ran back into the arms of the hunters.…

Anyway, he kept an eye open for good rocks as he made his way across to the tree, but there weren't any. How could he change the dream?… Before he'd thought of anything he reached the tree.

It was growing on a sloping slab of bedrock a bit taller than a man at its upper end. The tree roots ran down the face of the rock into the soil beneath. At the bottom lay a single chunk of rock, almost as large as Po's head, much too heavy for him to throw. It would have to do. The buck would just have to come nearer, so that he could drop the rock instead of throwing it. Why, he might even kill it, that way....

With a lot of effort he heaved the rock up into the tree and managed to wedge it into a fork. Then he found a place where he could perch in the shade of the trunk and start his watch.

Time passed. Po didn't mind. He had his dream to play with. It was a good dream, wonderful but not impossible, something he, Po, might really manage to do if he was very lucky.... There would be a feast that night, of course, and praise from the hunters, and he, Po, would be allowed to make his boast, and no one would laugh at him...and Nar would be watching with jealous eyes....

Something was happening!

Noises, a shout, men shouting, the shouts of the hunters as they leaped for the kill.

Po twisted around to where he could look toward the river, but could see nothing. The shouts were coming from down in the dry riverbed, out of sight. So the prey must have come from Nar's side, and he, Po, hadn't seen anything, nothing at all.... Surely his buck would break out now and come racing toward him....

No.

He turned back and stared longingly across the plain. Perhaps even now...

Far as the horizon nothing stirred on the baked and dreary emptiness, lit clear by the sideways light of the late-afternoon sun.

But yes, there!

Much closer than he'd been looking, a movement.

Why hadn't he seen it before?

Because it was almost the same color as the tawny plain. The lion-colored plain that hid the lions. But for the movement of their shadows he mightn't have seen them at all as they padded toward the river. Three lionesses and two cubs. Very dangerous.

A lioness with cubs to feed is afraid of nothing.

Po turned toward the river, cupped his hands around his mouth, and yelled the whooping, carrying call that meant *Danger!* Everyone used and understood it, both the

Moonhawks and the others from the old Kins, who had words, and the Porcupines, who didn't.

Nobody heard. The hunters were making too much noise. A few small deer were scrambling up the far bank and dashing off across the plain.

He called again, even louder. He saw the lions pause in their stride. Their heads turned toward him. His heart thumped. Lions could climb trees. He checked for a branch he could scramble along, too far for a lion to follow him. But the lions padded on toward the river.

Po waited for a lull in the shouting, and yelled again, *Danger!*

This time somebody heard him. A man appeared from the riverbed. He spotted the lions at once, now nearer to him than to Po's tree. He turned and shouted down to the other men in the riverbed. Several men scrambled up the far bank, three of them with the bodies of deer across their shoulders. They ran off, staggering under the weight, while the others followed as guards, looking over their shoulders as they ran.

That couldn't be everyone. No. As the two leading lions disappeared into the riverbed, more men climbed to the top of the farther bank. They all had rocks cradled on one arm, with the other one free for throwing. They lined up, ready to drive the lions back if they tried to attack.

A moment later two men came in sight to Po's left, farther up the riverbed, and started running toward him. He recognized Suth and Kern, and sighed with relief. They were coming to see that he was safe. Though he might dream of finding his own way back to the lair, alone in the dangerous night, he didn't want to have to do it for real.

But the lioness and her cubs hadn't yet followed the other two down into the riverbed. She too saw the men running toward the tree and at once turned and came after them at a rapid lope. The cubs followed.

Po yelled and pointed. The men glanced over their shoulders and sprinted for the tree. The lioness quickened her pace, gaining on them all the time.

Po scrambled around the tree to where he had wedged his rock, heaved it up and rested it at chest level on a sloping branch. Perhaps he could still do something. His heart hammered. This wasn't a dream.

Suth was faster than Kern. He reached the great boulder on which the tree stood and scrambled up it, then turned to help Kern.

Almost at the rock, Kern glanced back. As he did so, his foot caught, he stumbled and fell. He was up in an instant, but the lioness was close behind him. Suth shouted and flung his digging stick. Its sharpened end hit her on the right shoulder, below the neck, a good strong blow that made her flinch and pause a moment. Kern reached the boulder but hadn't time to climb it. Desperate, he put his back to it and raised his digging stick to strike one last blow.

Hopeless. This was a lioness with cubs to feed.

Po fought for a kneehold on the sloping branch. Two-handed, he heaved the rock above his head. He couldn't possibly throw it far enough. But perhaps, just as the lion sprang...

He tensed, scrabbling for a better hold, and slipped.

He grabbed for the branch, and the rock tumbled from his grasp. He watched it fall, straight down, useless.

It just missed Suth, slammed into the

very rim of the boulder, and shot forward, catching the lioness full in the face as she sprang. At the same moment Kern flung himself sideways. The lioness buffeted into the boulder and half fell, but staggered up, shaking her head, with blood streaming from her nose and mouth.

Suth yelled and helped Kern up the face of the boulder, and together they scrambled up the tree.

The lioness was still staggering around, trying to shake the blood off her face and out of her eyes, but after a little while she recovered enough to pause and study the three people in the tree. She and her cubs were scrawny with hunger. Every rib showed clearly. If she didn't find food soon they would all three die.

Po, Suth, and Kern watched her deciding whether to try to climb up after them. At last she turned and padded draggingly toward the river, followed by her cubs.

They waited until the lions vanished into the riverbed, then climbed down and ran off in the opposite direction before making their way back to the outcrop that was their lair. They took wide circuits around any cover that might hide other lions. By the time the outcrop came in sight their shadows stretched tens and tens of paces in front of them.

"Po," said Suth, when they were almost there, "tonight I tell the Kin your deed. I, Suth, praise."

"I, Kern, also praise," said Kern. "I praise and thank."

These were words that Po had longed to hear, ever since he could remember, especially from Suth. So why did they make him feel uncomfortable when they were now at last spoken? He didn't understand.

"The rock was big," said Kern wonderingly. "It was high in the tree. How is this?"

Suth looked at Po.

"I…I do not know," said Po. "I found it there."

He knew that Suth had long ago guessed about his dreams, but Po wasn't going to say anything about them in front of Kern.

"This was lucky, lucky," said Kern.

Suth was still looking at Po.

"Lucky is good, Po," he said.

Oldtale

The Daughters of Dat

Dat was of the Kin of Parrot. He had two daughters, children only, named Gata and Falu. Their mother, Pahi, was bitten by a red scorpion. At Ragala Flat she was bitten. There she died.

Dat said to his daughters, "I have no mate. Who now pounds grass seed for me? Who mixes gumroot paste? This is woman stuff."

Falu said, "We, your daughters, do these things, my father."

Gata said nothing.

Dat said, "One day men come,

from Fat Pig and from Weaver. They say to you, *Gata, Falu, we choose you for our mates. Do you choose us?* What then do you say to them?"

Falu said, "We say, *Go to our father, Dat. Ask him.*"

Dat said, "Is this a promise, my daughters?"

Falu said, "It is a promise, my father."

Gata said nothing.

So Gata and Falu did woman stuff for their father, Dat. They pounded his grass seed and mixed his gumroot paste. He was happy.

Tens of moons passed, and more tens, and Gata was almost a woman. Parrot camped at Stinkwater, and Snake was there also. Gata saw a young man, tall and strong. His name was Nal. She said to Falu, "Soon I am a woman. I choose Nal for my mate."

Falu said, "This is not good. You are Parrot, my sister. Nal is Snake."

Gata said, "These are words. I, Gata, choose Nal for my mate. I choose no other man."

Now Gata was a woman. She was very beautiful. Men came to her, from Fat Pig and from Weaver, and said, "Gata, we choose you for our mate. Choose one of us. Whom do you choose?"

Gata said, "My father, Dat, chooses for me. Ask him."

Gata whispered in her father's ear, "Choose none of these men, my father. I, Gata, ask."

Dat said to the men, "I choose none of you."

He was happy to do this. He did not wish Gata to leave him.

A new man came from Weaver. His name was Tov. He was small, but clever, and laughter was in his mouth.

Falu saw him. She was a child still, half-grown, but her heart sang for him. Tov saw only Gata. He came and came to Dat, saying, "Give me Gata for my mate."

Dat said to his daughters, "This man comes and comes. What do I say to him?"

Gata said, "Say this to him, my father: *First you give me a gift.*"

Dat said, "What gift do I ask?"

Gata said, "Say this to him, my father: *Bring me a tooth of the snake Fododo, the Father of Snakes. Bring me the poison tooth.*"

Dat said, "This is a hard thing I ask. Tov cannot do it."

Gata said, "You are right, my father. Tov cannot do it."

She laughed, and Dat laughed with her.

Tov came yet again to Dat. Falu saw him and followed him. She lay in long grasses and listened to their talk.

Tov said, "Give me Gata for my mate."

Dat said, "First you give me a gift. You give me a tooth of the snake Fododo, the Father of Snakes. You give me the poison tooth."

Tov laughed. He said, "You ask a hard thing. Yet for Gata I do it."

2

There was one good thing about the drought—fuel was easy to find. Most of the trees and bushes were dead. Dried by the roasting sun, their branches snapped off easily and then burst into flame at the first spark.

That night the people sat around the two fires they had built on the top of the outcrop where they were lairing. The moon was full, and the Kin were mostly Moonhawk, so they feasted. Not that it was much of a feast. They had three starved deer, a few small animals they'd hunted or trapped, some lizards and a couple of snakes, some wizened roots, a few handfuls of grubs, and sourgrass, whose leaves were good to chew but choked you if you tried to swallow them. That was all, but they'd eaten scraps of things during the day, and now everybody got three or four mouthfuls, so they finished hungry but not starving.

Kin—Po and the Moonhawks, and the remnants of other Kins who had straggled through to the New Good Places and joined them—sat around one fire, and the Porcupines around the other. This wasn't unfriendliness. They were on good terms and used to each other. Before the drought they had usually moved about separately, but when they'd met up they'd greeted each other with pleasure. Now, as the last water in the river failed, they were following it down together.

It was the only thing they could do. Already they had come almost as far as any of them had ever been, because to the north lay an enormous marsh, blocking their way. Po had heard the adults worrying about what they'd do when they reached it, but at least there ought to be water there.

The reason why Kin and Porcupines sat separate in the evenings was very simple. The Porcupines didn't have language. They touched and stroked each other much more than Kin did, and they used a lot of different sounds—warnings and commands and greetings and so on—but they couldn't talk about anything the way Kin did. They couldn't gossip or argue, or praise or boast, or tell and listen to the Oldtales, which was how Kin liked to spend their evenings.

Tor was the only Porcupine who stayed with the Moonhawks, because he was Moonhawk too. When Suth and Noli and Tinu had first rescued him, and Tinu had mended his broken arm, they had given him his name and let him join the Kin, and now he was Noli's mate. Po didn't remember the rescue. As far as he was concerned Tor had always been there, gentle and kindly, with his strange-shaped arm, because it had mended crooked, though it was perfectly strong.

They finished eating what little there was, but went on passing the meatless bones around to suck and gnaw in turn. While they were doing this, the men stood up and made their boasts about what they had done in the hunt.

Suth was the youngest of the men, so he came last. He stood and raised a hand for silence, and looked at Tun, who nodded. Though he was youngest, everyone listened when Suth spoke. They thought well of him.

When he was still a boy he had fought and killed a leopard, single-handed. That was a great deed, the deed of a hero. He had the scars of the leopard's claws on his left shoulder, and a small one on his cheek. The other men had man-scars on both cheeks, cut by the leader of their Kin at the special feast when they had been accepted as men. Suth had only the scar that the leopard had made. It was enough.

"I, Suth, speak praise," he began. "I praise the boy Po. We hunted. Po kept watch in a tree. Three lions came...."

Slowly he told the story—how he and Kern had run from the lioness, and how she had almost caught Kern, but Po, up in the tree, had thrown a great rock (Suth didn't say "dropped"—he said "threw") and had managed to stun the lioness long enough to let the two men climb the tree and escape.

Suth stopped and sat down. Po realized that everyone was looking at him, sitting with the women and children on the other side of the fire, opposite the men. Noli, beside him, nudged him gently with her elbow. He stood up and raised his arm and looked at Tun.

Tun nodded gravely. Silence fell. Po tried

to speak, to make his boast. This was a moment he'd dreamed of again and again, though boys didn't normally get to boast in front of all the adults like this—they boasted among themselves all the time, of course. In Po's dreams the words came smoothly, proudly. Not now. Whatever Suth said, he knew that he hadn't been the hero of his dreams, clever and brave, saving the day. Yes, he'd maybe saved Kern's life, but it had just been a stupid accident.

He gulped, and managed to speak.

"I, Po, did this. Yes. I did this. Suth said it. It is true. I…I…was lucky, lucky."

He sat down, almost weeping with shame at his stupid boast. Everyone was laughing. He bowed his head in misery. He longed to run away, away, far into the dark night. He felt Noli's arm slide around his shoulders.

"Po, why do you hide your head?" she whispered. "You do well, well. Suth praises you."

"They laugh at me," he muttered. "They laugh at my stupid words."

"No, Po," she said. "Your words are good. They are happy for you. They laugh. Listen. Now they laugh at Kern. It is different."

It was true. There was a new note in the

men's voices as they jeered at Kern for letting the lion almost catch him and needing a boy to save him.

"It is you, Kern, are lucky, lucky," they said.

"This is true," said Kern cheerfully.

Po felt better, but he stayed where he was, leaning against Noli, and she understood what he wanted and kept her arm comfortingly around him. Noli wasn't Po's mother—she was far too young—it was only eight moons since she and Tor had chosen each other for mates, and now she was fat with her first child inside her. But she had acted as mother to Po and Mana and her own small brother, Tan, since all their real parents had been killed or taken when savage strangers had attacked the Moonhawks and the other Kins and driven them out of their old Good Places.

Po couldn't remember any of that. He could just remember little bits of the time soon after, when the six of them—Suth, Noli, and Tinu, Po himself, and Mana and Tan, who had been called Otan then because he was still a baby—had lived for a while with the lost Monkey Kin in a hidden valley at the top of a mountain. He knew the mountain had exploded. He'd been told about that, but all he could remember was running desperately up a rocky slope in the dark and clutching something he'd been told to keep hold of while rocks rained down all around him and a huge hot orange mass roared and boomed below.

He didn't remember a lot that had happened after that, like meeting the Porcupines—Suth said that had been in a canyon somewhere—and then coming to the New Good Places and finding Tun and Kern and Chogi and the rest of the Moonhawks.

All Po's real memories were about living in the New Good Places, along with the people who now sat around the two fires. But he still thought of the five who'd done the things he'd been told about as his own family. Suth was father and Noli was mother, although Suth was mated with Bodu and they had their own baby son, Ogad, and Noli's baby would be born inside a moon.

Tinu was a big sister, or maybe an aunt, though she wasn't a woman yet. And Mana was Po's younger sister, and Tan was his little brother, though really they'd all had different parents. So Po felt closer to these

five than he did to anyone else on the outcrop. Just now he was sitting between Noli
and Mana, with Tinu on Noli's other side.
Tan was running around between the two
fires, playing tag with other small boys, both
Kin and Porcupines. You didn't need words
to play tag.

While the men were still teasing Kern,
Chogi stood up and crossed to the other side
of the fire and faced Tun. She bent her
knees and dipped her head briefly and made
a fluttering movement in the air with her
fingers. Chogi was senior woman. Nobody
expected her to kneel right down and patter
her hands on the ground in front of the
leader, as a junior woman would have done.

"Chogi, we listen," said Tun.

Chogi dipped her head again and moved
slowly to the gap between the men's side
and the women's, so that everybody could
see and hear her. It was obvious that she had
something important to say.

She was a short, wrinkle-faced woman. Po
had never seen her laugh. He could remember when she'd been rather fat, but now she
was skinny with hunger, like everybody else.
Her main business was to see that the Kin
kept strictly to their ancient customs, stuff

to do with childbirth and choosing mates, and things that were done when babies became small ones, or small ones became children, or children became men and women. Po thought this sort of thing very dull, so instead of listening to Chogi he started dreaming his boast over, with him, Po, saying the words he wished he'd said. While he was at it he went back and changed the actual adventure, so that he'd found a couple of good throwing rocks on his way to the tree....

Something was happening. The men had stopped whispering among themselves as they usually did when woman stuff was being discussed. Po came out of his dream and listened.

"The moon is big," Chogi was saying. "We feast. This is good. This is happy time. But now we go to new places, dangerous, dangerous. Do we find food? Do we feast again? When is another happy time? I do not know. So I, Chogi, say this. We do happy-time stuff now. We do it here. I see Nar. I see Tinu. Soon Nar is a man. Soon Tinu is a woman. Soon they choose mates. Nar chooses Tinu. There is no other woman. Tinu chooses Nar. There is no other man. They smear salt on their foreheads. This is good. It is happy-time stuff. So I, Chogi, say they do not wait. They do this now. I, Chogi, say this."

She stopped but stayed where she was, with the firelight wavering across her old, lined face, and the big moon halfway up the sky behind her. Everyone seemed too surprised to speak. Even Po understood that what Chogi was suggesting was a break with custom. No one had been surprised when Suth and Bodu had chosen each other. There hadn't been anyone else for them to choose, and besides, Bodu was from Little Bat, which was one of the two Kins from which Moonhawk men were allowed to choose.

Even so, they'd waited until they'd both been through the correct customs for becoming man and woman. Then, at a full-moon feast, they had stood up from each side of the fire and crossed to the place where Chogi now stood, and touched palms, and said the words of choosing, and smeared salt on their foreheads, just as Nal and Turka had done long, long ago, at the first ever such choosing, by the saltpans beyond

Lusan of the Ants—one of the old Good Places, where none of them would ever go again.

Now chatter broke out as everybody began to talk about Chogi's idea. Even the men were interested. It wasn't just the business of Nar and Tinu choosing each other before they were man and woman. Nar was Monkey. He and his mother, Zara, had somehow escaped when the mountain where Monkey used to live had exploded. There'd been other people with them, but they'd all died, wandering lost in a desert somewhere. Only Zara had struggled through with her small son, Nar, and come at last to the New Good Places and joined up with the Moonhawks. Now they were the last of the Monkey Kin, and nobody knew who Monkey were allowed to mate with.

The adults thought this sort of thing was very important, though as far as Po could see it didn't make much sense any more. Who was he supposed to choose when his turn came? The only girls the right age were Mana, who was Moonhawk (Chogi wouldn't like that at all), and Sibi, who would be almost a small one still, and besides that she was Parrot, and Moonhawk wasn't allowed to mate with Parrot—and anyway Sibi made it obvious she thought Po was stupid.

Po leaned forward and looked to see how Tinu was taking Chogi's suggestion, but she'd shrunk back into Noli's shadow with her hands over her face—her strange, twisted mouth always made her try to hide like that when anyone drew attention to her. Po hoped she didn't like the idea. He didn't want Nar becoming part of his family, the way Tor and Bodu were now.

Po didn't really have any good reason for making Nar his enemy. Nar was just another boy, a bit older than Po himself. Perhaps they should have been friends. There were no other boys anywhere near their age among the Kin. Nar was taller and stronger than Po, but that was just because he was older—and he wasn't a bully or a loud-mouth. Other people seemed to like him, but that only made it worse.

The real reason why Po didn't like Nar was his smile. Nar smiled a lot, almost whenever anybody spoke to him, and when Po made one of his boasts—claiming he'd done something he hadn't really, or promis-ing he would when everyone knew he couldn't—Nar smiled that smile and looked at him for a moment, a look that said, "I am almost a man, and you are nothing but a stupid little boy...."

Po stood up, pretending he needed a stretch and a yawn but really to get a look at Nar and see how he was reacting. He couldn't see him. Where was he? Ah, that must be him, just beyond Zara, but Po couldn't see his face. Zara was saying something to him. He must have answered, because she shook her head and made a furious gesture with her left hand, as if she were trying to sweep the whole idea away.

Great—Zara didn't want it to happen either. Po couldn't imagine that Tinu really wanted Nar for her mate. Chogi was just a silly old woman. Why didn't Tun stand up and say so?...

As he settled down again, Po realized that something was happening to Noli, beside him. She was shuddering, and breathing in slow, deep lungfuls. Now her body went stiff. Her eyes were open, but rolled so far up that he could see only white below the bulging lids. Froth gathered at the corners of her mouth.

Po wasn't alarmed. He understood what

was happening, and was ready when Noli took an even deeper breath and shot suddenly to her feet. She didn't scramble awkwardly up, as she usually did now because the baby inside her unbalanced her. This time it was more as if something had taken hold of her and just jerked her upright.

Everybody stopped talking and looked at her. None of this was strange to them. They waited in silence.

She raised her arms and stood as still as a tree. Then a voice came out of her, not her own voice, not any man's or woman's, but a big, soft voice like an echo from a cave, the voice of Moonhawk, the First One.

"Wait," said the voice. "It is not the time."

As the last whisper of the voice faded into the night, Noli crumpled. This sometimes happened, so Po was already kneeling, ready to catch her, but she went the other way, into Tinu's arms, and now by the firelight Po could see Tinu's face. Her twisted mouth was open, with her jaw working sideways and down as if she'd gotten something stuck there. Her cheeks were streaming with tears.

Mana had seen too. By the time Po had

helped ease Noli down onto the rock, Mana was kneeling on Tinu's other side with both arms around her, hugging her close. Tinu huddled beside Noli's sleeping body with her head in her hands, sobbing bitterly. Po moved around to hug her from the other side.

"Do not weep, Tinu," he begged her. "Why do you weep?"

Mana made a face at him to be quiet, but Tinu answered, mumbling through her sobs.

"No man…chooses…Tinu…. No man… ever."

Po, desperate to comfort her, said the first thing that came into his head.

"I find a mate for you, Tinu. I, Po, do this."

She took her hands away from her face and looked at him, and he could see that she was trying to smile, but the tears still streamed down. Mana, behind Tinu's shoulder, was frowning at him, shaking her head. He sighed and moved back to the other side of Noli's sleeping body and sat with his chin on his fists, staring at the small, wavering flames as they danced over the heap of glowing embers.

What had he said wrong? What did Tinu

mean, saying no one would ever choose her for a mate? There wasn't anything wrong with Tinu, anything that mattered. Her face wasn't like other people's, with its broken, twisted look, and she couldn't talk right. But she did have language—you just had to get used to the mumbling way she spoke. And she was clever, clever with her mind and her hands. She sometimes found good new ways of doing things, which people had never thought of.

Anyway, he told himself, as soon as she was a woman some man was going to choose her for a mate. What man? As Chogi had said, there wasn't anyone except Nar. Forget about Nar. He, Po, was going to find someone.

Oldtale

Falu's Prayer

Falu said to Gata, "Stay with my father. Pound grass seed. Mix bloodroot paste."

Gata said, "My sister, where do you go?"

Falu said, "I follow Tov. He seeks the tooth of Fododo, Father of Snakes. Tov is clever. Perhaps he gets the tooth. But I set traps in his path. I lead him astray."

Gata said, "My sister, this is good."

Falu went first to Dindijji, the place of dust trees. As she went, she gathered nuts. She dug gum root from the ground and chewed it and spat the chewings into her gourd.

She came to Dindijji. She made paste from her chewings and spread it on a rock in the sun. Soon it was very sticky. She smeared it on the branches of the dust trees, and so stuck the nuts to them.

Parrots came to eat the nuts, the little gray parrots with the yellow tail feathers. They stuck to the paste. Falu caught them. From each she took a yellow tail feather.

She gave nuts to them and set them free.

She said, "Little gray parrots, fly to the First One. Say to him, *Falu is our friend. She gives nuts to us.*"

She stuck feathers to her buttocks, the yellow tail feathers. She rolled herself beneath the trees, and poured their dust over her head, the gray dust. She said, "Now I am a parrot, a little gray parrot with yellow tail feathers."

At nightfall she climbed a tree. To its topmost branches she climbed. The little gray parrots came and roosted around her. They woke at the sunrise and flew hither and thither and sang their song. It was the time of the parrots.

Falu sang also. These words she sang:

Parrot, First One.
I am your nestling.
You brood over me.
You bring me sweet fruits.
Give me Tov for my mate.

Five nights Falu stayed in the tree, neither eating nor drinking. Each morning she sang with the parrots.

On the sixth night she bound herself around with tingin bark and slept. The tingin bark held her safe.

Falu dreamed. Parrot came to her in her dream and said, "Falu, you are my nestling. I brood over you. I bring you sweet fruits. I give you Tov for your mate. Go where he goes."

Falu woke in the morning. She looked at her arms, and they were wings. She looked at her fingers, and they were the gray feathers of the wing tips.

Her chin itched. She scratched it with her foot. She looked at the foot, and it was the foot of a bird.

She opened her mouth and sang. Her voice was the voice of a parrot.

Falu said in her heart, *This is good. I go where Tov goes. He does not know me.*

3

There was no food left where they were, so the next day they moved on north. To search a wider area, the Porcupines stayed on the east side of the river and the Moonhawks crossed to the west. It was hard going. The land became more and more like true desert. The trees along the river that used to be green all year were mostly leafless and dead. Water was hard to find, even when they dug in the riverbed, and they were lucky if they each got a few mouthfuls of food a day.

For several days they moved on like that. Hunger seemed to follow Po like his own shadow. He was hungry even in his dreams. Soon he was thirsty too. They could smell the water trickling below the riverbed, but when they dug down they found almost none there. They sucked pebbles and chewed dry sticks to give their mouths something to do.

The women were very anxious about the babies, both Bodu's little Ogad and Noli's unborn child. Was Bodu getting enough food to make good milk? Was Noli getting enough to make the baby grow inside her? Would she have milk to feed it when it was born? They gave the two mothers everything they could spare, but it wasn't really enough.

The men were worried too. Po heard some of them talking together one evening after they'd had a stroke of luck and found a patch of good gourds, the sort that would hold water for several moons without going soft, once they'd been well salted and smoked. The men were working at this, while the women prepared the scraps of food that had been found.

"We use all the salt," said Var. "It is gone. Now we go far and far. Do we find more salt? Do we find cutter stones? Do we find tingin trees?"

He spoke gloomily. Var was like that, but this time the other men grunted in agreement. These were all things that people used every day. You couldn't make a good digging stick without a cutter, or loops to carry a gourd without tingin bark, and salt was useful for preventing meat from rotting and for making food taste better. But all these things were scarce too. You could go many days' journey without finding them.

"There is a salt pan out there," said Net, jumping up and pointing west, as if he was ready to start out that moment. "Yova found it. It has no name."

"It is too far," said Tun. "There is no food there. No Good Place. Not any more. It is gone."

Po knew what they were talking about. He could just remember the times before the rains had begun to fail, when they'd been able to roam over a much wider tract of land, going from one Good Place to another. Now all the Good Places had been swallowed up by the desert.

He stopped listening to the talk and started on a dream in which he, Po, sneaked off secretly into the dark, traveling by the light of the moon, and after several good adventures reached the salt pan Yova had found and dug out a slab of wonderful white salt, the best sort, so white that it glittered in the moonlight. Then he journeyed home with it and sneaked into the camp while the others still slept, and when they woke in the morning they found it by the embers of the fire and couldn't imagine how it came there. And then he, Po, told them.

It was a good dream. Po was still working on it when they all lay down to sleep.

The next few days were worse. The river split up into a maze of smaller rivers, all dry now, separated by islands and mudbanks and immense tangles of dead reed, the kind of dangerous, useless territory that Kin called demon places. Somewhere over on the far side were the Porcupines—there'd been no sign of them for several days and they were now quite out of reach.

Water was still hard to find. Sometimes they had to wait all morning before they could move on, while a few of the adults fought their way through with the empty gourds and came back with the stinking, muddy liquid.

Several people fell sick. Mana was the worst. She staggered, so that Po had to put his arm around her and help her along. And she was hot and cold by turns and babbled about things that weren't there.

And then Cal was stung on the foot by a scorpion. His whole leg swelled up. He was a brave man, but he howled and wept with the pain of it, and they thought he was going to die. But by the next morning the pain and the swelling were almost gone, and then the leg shriveled to a stick, so that he walked with a heavy limp.

Po didn't go to search for water, of course. He tried a couple of dreams about doing it, but the demons got into them, and they scared him.

They reached the main marshes very weak and depressed. This was as far as any of them had ever been, even before the rains had failed. They halted at the top of a low rise and looked north.

It was evening, and beyond the first few tens of paces everything was hidden under a strange haze, golden with the light of the setting sun. It didn't seem to be very dense. Po could see the first few mudbanks and reed patches clearly enough, but then they became vague, blurred shapes, and then vanished completely. There was no sign of a pathway, and it was too late to explore, so they made camp and slept.

When they woke in the morning the haze

had cleared, and they could see what they were in for.

The marshes were demon places, too. Po hadn't known what to expect, so he'd made them up in his mind, mudbanks and tall green reeds with patches of clear water between them. The reeds were there, a vast brown tangle. The mud was there, dried and cracked. There was no water. Insects swarmed out of the reeds and gathered around the newcomers. Po couldn't see how far the marsh stretched, but beyond it, almost as blue as the glaring blue sky, he could see a wavering line which he knew was distant hills.

Suth pointed.

"We go there," he said. "See, it rains. We find Good Places there."

Po looked, and yes, in the far distance he could see two separate dark masses of rain cloud blurring the horizon.

"Suth, we cannot cross the marsh," said Bodu.

She spoke dismally. Usually she was cheerful. Po liked her. She laughed at him sometimes, but she didn't make it sound jeering or scornful—she just liked to laugh. But she was worried about her baby, Ogad, who wasn't yet three moons old. He was very thin and fretful, because she hadn't enough milk to give him. If Bodu didn't find better food soon, Ogad would die.

Po longed to comfort her. As usual he spoke before he thought.

"I find a way through the marshes," he said. "I, Po, do this."

Behind him someone laughed, and he swung around. It was Nar, not trying to hide his smile. Po took a pace toward him and stuck his chin out. He felt his scalp stir as it tried to make his hair bush out, though he'd have to be a man before that would happen so that anyone could see.

"I, Po, speak, Nar," he snapped. "I find the way through the marshes. Does Nar say *No* to me?"

Nar wasn't impressed. His smile widened.

"You do this, Po," he said. "Then I give you a gift."

"What gift, Nar?"

Po was really angry. He thought he could feel his hair actually moving a little.

"You ask, I give," said Nar carelessly, making it yet more obvious he was sure Po couldn't do what he'd promised. All this was man stuff, the sort of words Var and

Kern might have used in an argument. The boys copied the men, of course. For them it was a kind of game. Po could see that was how Nar was treating it this time.

Po wasn't. He looked around and saw a boulder jutting up out of the ground a few paces behind Nar.

"Come," he said, and marched over to it, not looking to see if Nar followed.

He did, and he wasn't smiling now.

Po laid his right hand on the boulder.

"This is the rock Odutu…" he began, but Nar interrupted him.

"Po, I take back my words," he said.

"You say I, Po, find the way through the marshes?"

"No, Po," said Nar quietly. "You do not do this thing. You do not try. It is dangerous, dangerous."

But Po was much too angry to listen, either to the words or the way in which Nar had spoken them. He put his hand back on the rock.

"This is the rock Odutu, Odutu below the Mountain," he said. "On Odutu I say this. *I, Po, find the way through the marshes.*"

He stood back and waited. This was the strongest oath or challenge anyone knew.

Odutu was a real place, a huge rock, far in the south of the old Good Places, standing at the foot of the mountain where the First Ones lived. Po had been taken there when he was a small one, but he didn't remember. All he knew was an Oldtale that said that an oath sworn at Odutu was an oath for ever. Since they were all now so far away from the real Odutu, any big rock would do almost as well, provided the right words were used.

Nar hesitated, sighed, and shrugged. He put his hand on the boulder and muttered, "This rock is Odutu, Odutu below the Mountain. On Odutu I say this. *Po finds the way through the marsh, then I give him a gift. Po asks. I, Nar, give.*"

He looked at Po and shook his head disapprovingly, but without saying a word went back and joined the others.

Po followed. Nobody seemed to have noticed what they were up to. They were just a couple of boys doing boy stuff, and there was something more interesting happening in the other direction.

The solid ground ended in a low bank, and then the marsh began. Everyone was lined up along the bank watching someone—Net, of course, he always rushed into things—picking his way across a patch of dried mud between two tangles of reeds, moving a half pace at a time and testing the surface beneath each foot before he shifted his weight onto it. He was four or five paces from the bank when the surface gave way.

At once he was right in to his waist, but the sticky black mud seemed to be deeper than that, and he went on sinking as he floundered around and tried to wade back.

Soon he was up to his chest, struggling frantically for the bank but not getting any nearer. Everyone was shouting. The other men were down at the edge of the marsh, Tun giving orders.

Suth started to crawl out onto the mud. He was the lightest of the men. Now he lay on his belly and wormed his way forward, spreading his weight across the treacherous mud. Po watched with his heart in his mouth.

As soon as Suth's feet were clear of the bank, Var kneeled and gripped his ankles, and then as Suth moved farther out, Var too lay down and wormed after him, while Kern and Tor kneeled and held Var's ankles. By the time Suth could grasp Net's wrists, Net was up to his neck, Suth and Var were well out on the mud, and Tor and Kern were kneeling and leaning out over it to keep hold of Var.

The angle was awkward. Neither of the two on solid ground could pull with any strength, and the two out on the mud didn't dare risk pulling at all. But now, without waiting for Tun to give the order, the women formed two lines, each with her arms around the one in front of her, and the two at the head of the lines gripping Tor and Kern around their waists.

Chogi called, and they heaved, all together. Suth and Var took the strain. Po could see the muscles of their forearms bulging as they fought to keep their grip. Net stopped sinking. The women heaved rhythmically, Tun calling the time. It wasn't enough. Net remained stuck fast. Po and Nar and the older children joined the ends of the lines and added their weight. Po was well up the bank and could still see the men out on the mud.

The surface under Suth gave way but somehow he kept his hold, turning his head sideways to keep his nose and mouth clear while he floated on the filthy ooze. The changed angle must have helped. Slowly, so slowly that Po could hardly see it was happening, Var's feet were coming closer to the bank. The bodies of Tor and Kern were straightening. Net's shoulders were clear of the mud.

And then he came with a rush. The teams on the bank fell over backward. By the time they were on their feet, Tor and Kern were hauling Var ashore and Suth and Net were slithering back over the surface. And then they were on firm ground, and everyone was crowding around them, shouting with triumph and jeering at Net for his rashness, while they tried to scrape the stinking mud off their bodies.

But Po stayed at the top of the bank, staring out over the marsh, with dismay in his heart.

Not that way, he thought. Not even in dreams.

Oldtale
Gogoli

Tov went to Fon, his father's father. He was very old, and knew many things.

Tov said, "Father of my father, old Fon, tell me this. Where is the lair of Fododo, Father of Snakes?"

Fon said, "Tov, son of my son, no man knows this. Only one knows this. He is Gogoli, the Jackal Who Knows All Things."

Tov said, "Where is Gogoli?"

Fon said, "He is here, he is there. But at little moon he drinks at the water hole beyond Ramban. He does not drink, then he dies."

Tov said, "I thank Fon, father of my father."

Fon said, "Tov, son of my son, be lucky."

Then Fon died. He was very old.

Tov journeyed to Ramban. There he saw a parrot, a little gray parrot with yellow tail feathers. He said, "Why is this parrot here? Its place is at Dindijji, the place of dust trees. Surely Gata sends it. Her Kin is Parrot."

He laughed. The parrot answered, and its voice was laughter.

Tov said, "Parrot, we are two who laugh. Come with me. You are my guide."

At that the parrot flew down and sat upon his head.

It was the night of little moon, so Tov journeyed to the water hole beyond Ramban. He saw a wingnut tree beside the path and said, "This is good. I lie in wait behind this tree. Gogoli comes. I leap out. I catch him. Parrot, fly into the tree. Keep watch with me. Make no noise."

Tov lay by the path and waited. At dusk Gogoli came. Many people hunted Gogoli, to steal his knowledge. So he made a magic as he went, a sleep magic. The hunters slept and did not catch him.

Now Gogoli made his magic, and Tov slept.

The parrot did not sleep. It was not people. When it saw Gogoli, it flew down and cried in Tov's ear. He woke and leaped up.

Gogoli fled, but Tov caught him by the tail. He tied tingin bark to the tail and hauled Gogoli up into the tree.

Gogoli said, "Man, let me go. This night I drink at the water hole. I do not drink, then I die."

Tov said, "Tell me this first. I seek Fododo, Father of Snakes. Where is his lair?"

Gogoli said, "It is in the desert, where no man goes. It is west from Tarutu Rock, three days. It is north a half day."

Tov said, "Where is there water on the way?"

Gogoli said, "Twoheads has water. It is beneath him. Bagworm has water. It is there, and not there. Stonejaw has water. It is inside him."

Tov said, "Last, tell me this. I seek the tooth of Fododo, the poison tooth. How must I steal it?"

At that Gogoli was very angry. He said, "How can I know this? No man has done it. It is a thing not known."

Then Tov untied the tingin bark and Gogoli went to the water hole and drank. But his sleep magic was still strong, and Tov lay down and slept.

Now it was dark, and the parrot was people again. It was Falu.

Falu said in her heart, *Gogoli's magic is strong, strong. Perhaps danger comes. Tov does not wake. Now I, Falu, keep watch.*

So Falu watched all night. She did not sleep. In the morning she was a parrot again.

Tov woke. He said, "Little gray parrot, I dreamed. In my dream I slept. One kept watch. It was a woman. My thought is, *It was Gata.*"

The parrot answered. Its voice was laughter.

4

There was nothing to do but turn westward and try to find a way around the marsh. As the sun rose higher the mudbanks began to steam, and soon everything beyond the first few tens of paces was again hidden in haze. Sometimes a pool of water between the mudbanks reached as far as the dry ground, so at least there was enough to drink. But there was no food at all, only the reeds and the mud and the dry, dry land.

So they trudged along all day, with despair in everyone's heart. Soon clouds of insects found and followed them, so they moved a little inland to be free of the worst of them. Tun was already looking for a place to camp when Po noticed Moru heading off by herself to the right. For something to do, he trotted after her.

"Moru, where do you go?" he asked.

"I go see," she said. "Perhaps we are lucky."

She smiled her thin smile. Moru was one of the stragglers who had come back with Tun when he had gone to see if there was anyone left in the old Good Places. Her Kin was Little Bat, but her mate was dead, and so was Var's, so they had chosen each other. But Po felt that she always had a sad look because of everything that had happened to her.

Just before she reached the edge of the marsh she stopped and crouched down. Here the solid ground didn't end in a bank, but in a large, gently sloping patch of soft, sandy dirt. With a grunt of satisfaction Moru walked a couple of paces forward, crouched again, and gently scooped the dirt aside. Po watched over her shoulder.

She grunted again, scooped even more gently, and then carefully lifted something free and showed it to Po. It was a large egg.

"What bird makes this?" he asked, astonished.

"It is not bird. It is turtle," said Moru. "We, Little Bat, had a Good Place. It was at Sometimes River. There were turtle nests. Look, here are many. Call the others."

Po ran up the slope, hallooed, and beckoned. Heads turned.

"Come. Moru finds food," he called, and they all came running. Moru showed them how to look, and in the end they found ten and ten and two more nests, all full of eggs with little baby turtles almost ready to hatch. They carried them well away from the marsh and built a good fire of dead branches and roasted the eggs on the embers. It was the best feast they'd had for several moons.

But the next three days were very bad. They found only two patches of water they could reach, and almost no food at all. On the third day the ground rose, and they walked endlessly along a barren, rocky slope above the marshes. By afternoon even the usually cheerful Kern was looking dismal, and poor Bodu was weeping with anxiety over her baby. Po was too sick-hearted to dream.

Then, when the sun was low in the west, he felt a faint breeze blowing in his face, with a new smell in it. Water. Not the dead, stinking water of the marsh, but sweet, clean water with green plants growing in and around it.

Everyone smelled it at the same moment. Their weary legs found strength. The loads they were carrying seemed suddenly lighter. Their pace quickened. Some of the men loped ahead. Po saw them turn and shout and wave, black spindly shapes against the glare of sunset. Most of the party broke into a run, but Noli was very tired after walking all day with her baby inside her, and by now Suth and Tor were helping her along, so Po stayed too. They came up with the others last of all, and saw what they had found.

It was a true Good Place, like the ones that Po could only just remember, before the rains had failed. A narrow strip of the marshes ran south into the desert, but this was a different kind of marshes, with good clear pools and banks of tall green reeds, and leafy bushes growing along the shore-lines. Surely there was food there, as well as water.

Hungry and thirsty though they were, they didn't rush down, but stood and looked around for possible dangers. Then Tun pointed to a place where open ground reached down to the water between two patches of bushes. He set lookouts in every direction before he and a few of the adults went to refill the water gourds.

Po was told to watch back the way they had come, but hardly had he taken up his post when he heard a yell from behind him, one voice, then several, screaming, *Danger! Run!* He turned to look. People were racing away from the water. Beyond them something large and dark and glistening was hurtling up the slope. For a moment he couldn't see it properly. A scream rose above the yells. Someone had fallen down.

As the others stopped running and turned back to help, Po saw the creature clearly.

Crocodiles didn't come that big!

Po could remember crocodiles basking on the sandbanks of the river when it had still run through the New Good Places, ugly creatures with thick, scaly hides and long snouts full of jagged teeth. He'd been smaller then, and they'd seemed huge to him, but he knew that they'd really been only two or three paces long, at the most.

This one was more than twice that. It was a monster, a nightmare, a demon from the Oldtales.

He watched it shy away as the people rushed shouting toward it. The men struck at it with their digging sticks as it hummocked itself down to the water. It seemed not to feel their blows. As it slid beneath the surface, Po saw that it had something in its mouth.

Now the people were coming slowly back up from the water. Po could feel their shock and horror. Four of the men were carrying somebody cradled between them. When they reached the crest where Po and the others were waiting, they laid him on the ground. It was Cal. His left leg, the one that had been stung by the scorpion, was gone, bitten clean off just above the knee. He had fainted. Chogi was trying to staunch the blood flow with her hands, but it pulsed violently out between her fingers.

Po couldn't bear to watch, so he stared out over the desert. Still nothing moved there, so he turned again and gazed down at the peaceful-seeming stretch of water below, all pink and golden under the sunset. His thirst was suddenly so fierce that he barely noticed when Chogi said, "Cal is dead. He is gone."

Everyone groaned, but still Po could think of nothing but his thirst.

"Tonight we mourn for Cal," said Tun.

"Now we fill our gourds. This is dangerous, dangerous. First, I do it. Then others, by one and by one."

Again Po was set to keep lookout, but he kept glancing over his shoulder to see what was happening. One by one the adults dashed down to different places on the bank to fill the gourds, while the others showered rocks and lumps of dirt into the water to scare attackers away. Nothing happened, and after a short time they returned to the ridge with brimming gourds.

Everyone had a drink, and then, still keeping careful watch and staying well away from the water's edge, they used the last of daylight to explore for food. To their delight they found several patches of dinka and one of thornfruit. Dinka was a small bush whose young leaves tasted of nothing much but could be swallowed after a lot of chewing. Thornfruit was a sort of cactus with vicious spines. The fruits were tricky to pick, and poisonous raw, but well roasted on embers they became sweet and juicy.

When it was almost dark they carried what they'd found back up the hillside and built their fire and made camp. After they'd eaten Tun stood and raised his hand for silence.

"We mourn for Cal," he said. "He is dead."

The women rose and stood in a line on their side of the fire. The children moved back to give them room. The men, sitting cross-legged opposite them, started to beat out the rhythm with their hands. But before the dance could begin, Po saw Noli stiffen and then walk with slow, jerky steps, as if something were moving her from outside, to the gap between the two groups. The men stopped clapping and waited. Noli closed her eyes, and when Moonhawk's voice came out of her it spoke so softly that Po could only just hear the words.

"Fat Pig is dead. He is gone," said the voice.

It was the saddest sound Po had ever heard.

Noli bowed her head. For a long while nobody moved or spoke, and then she opened her eyes and moved quietly back to her place in the line.

"Cal was Fat Pig," said Chogi. "He was the last. There are no more Fat Pig."

Even Po, who didn't often think about such things, felt the solemnity of the moment. The Kins had always been there, ever since the time of the Oldtales. There'd been eight of them (or nine, counting Monkey, but Monkey was different). Now... now, really, there was only one, Po's own Kin, Moonhawk. Moonhawk and a few scraps. There was nobody from Weaver in the group around the fire, and nobody from Ant Mother. As far as anyone knew, those Kins were dead too, gone. But Cal's death was the first time anyone had actually been there at the moment when a Kin vanished.

Tun gave the signal, the men clapped the rhythm, and the women shrilled the death wail and danced the dance—three stamps of the right foot and three stamps of the left, again and again and again—while the sparks wavered up above the embers of the fire toward the star-filled sky. Mana, sitting beside Po, took his hand. He looked at her and saw she was weeping, so he put his arm around her and held her close.

Po didn't feel like weeping but he felt very strange, not like Po at all, but like somebody much older, much more wise and serious. This person didn't think about Po stuff. He thought about time, and the people who'd been alive once and weren't any more—all those lives, those ancestors, going back and back and back to the time of the Oldtales, all who had ever been Kin, come down to these few living people left around their fire in the desert.

And they were alive only by the skin of their teeth. If they hadn't found this Good Place, then tomorrow, perhaps, or the day after, Moonhawk would have been gone too, like Weaver, like Ant Mother, like Fat Pig. No Moonhawk, not any more, ever….

From where he was sitting, if he looked to his right, Po could see out over the marshes. The haze that had hidden them all day had gone. What he saw was an immense dark distance, ending in a range of hills outlined against the paler sky. Over there, the rains had not failed; over there were Good Places where Moonhawk could live and thrive, more lives and yet more lives, going on and on through time….

It had to be true.

If only they could get there.

———

The next morning, they filled their gourds in the same way as they had the evening before, some darting in one at a time to different places on the shoreline, while others showered the surface with clods and stones. Po and the children watched tensely until it was over, but there was no sign of the monster, or of any smaller crocodiles.

Next, according to their custom, they carried Cal's body well away into the desert and mourned again and left it there with his gourd and digging stick and a cutter.

Then they returned to the inlet and explored this new Good Place, foraging as they went. They found plant food, dinka leaves and whitestem and thornfruit, and a bluish root called ran-ran, and various seeds, a far better harvest than they'd gathered anywhere for the last several moons. Even the swarming insects seemed somehow less horrible than in the main marsh. There were plenty of birds deep in the dense thickets, and tracks of small animals beneath them, but no sign of anything larger. Po heard some of the men talking about this.

"This is strange," said Kern, who was the best tracker among the men. "Here is food. Here is water. I see deer tracks. I see pig tracks. They are old, old. None are new."

"I see no swimming birds," said Net.

"The crocodile eats them," said Var gloomily. The other two laughed, because that was the sort of thing Var always said, but a little later, while Po was hunting for a way into a cactus thicket to reach a juicy-looking thornfruit, he heard a call of "Tun, come look!"

It was Kern's voice. Po forgot about the thornfruit and scampered along to see what was up. He found the men looking at one of the patches of open ground that ran right down to the water's edge. Kern was kneeling and pointing at what he'd seen.

"These tracks are old, old," he was saying. "Two moons? Three? I do not know. See, five deer come. Two are young. They are slow, careful. And see there, they run, four only. One is young. They run fast, fast. Now see here...."

He moved nearer to the water and pointed at an area where the two lines of hoof-prints suddenly disappeared, as if a huge fist had been rubbed over the place, wiping them out. Kern pointed at a pattern of dimples amid the mess, and with his forefinger outlined the shape of a large round foot with four spread toes.

"Crocodile," he said. "Big, big. Deer go to drink. Crocodile comes from the water. It takes one deer, a young one. See, it drags it...."

He pointed to a groove in the dirt, running all the way down to the water. Everyone gazed out over the peaceful surface. Po saw Yova stiffen, then slowly raise her hand and point.

"See, by the reeds," she said quietly. "Eight paces from the edge. It watches."

Po stared, trying to see what Yova had noticed. There was a stand of tall green reeds close to the shore. He looked along its edge. How far was eight paces?... Yes! There! Where that reed had twitched with nothing to stir it! Light ripples were spreading away from a small patch of what looked like floating mud and reed leaf that was drifting very gently toward the shore.

In an instant, with a thud of the heart, Po's way of seeing it changed, so that it wasn't a patch of mud but the very top of a crocodile's head. The slight mound at the near end was the nostrils, and the one at the back was the eye ridge. Po could see the glisten of a watching eye.

He shuddered and drew back. He wasn't

the only one; in fact most were already moving when the crocodile attacked.

It burst out in a sudden violent surge, its tail lashing the water to foam, and rushed toward them. They fled, scattering right and left. Po risked a glance over his shoulder and saw that the crocodile wasn't pursuing them, but had halted just about where they'd been standing. He stopped and turned, waiting to see what it would do next. He was sure it was the one they'd seen last night—there couldn't be two that huge. The people were scattered up the slope, some still running, others, like Po, standing to watch, but all tense and ready to run again.

The crocodile rested only a moment or two before starting another charge, hummocking its body up and driving itself forward with its stubby back legs. Again everyone scattered. This time when Po glanced back, the monster was still pursuing, and gaining on him. With horror he realized that it was actually faster than he was. Desperately he raced on and stopped only when he saw Chogi, just ahead of him, look back, and halt and turn.

He turned and stood, with his heart

pounding. The crocodile had halted again, halfway up from the inlet. As he watched, it raised its head and gave a deep, thundering roar, unlike any animal Po had ever heard.

Net answered with a shout, dashed forward, and flung his digging stick. It was a well-aimed shot, but the stick bounced off the animal's hide like a twig. It swung around and lurched toward Net, forcing him back. Others copied him, still not doing any harm, but after a while the crocodile seemed to realize it wasn't going to catch anyone this time. It turned, dragged itself back into the water, and disappeared. A little later they saw it climb out onto a small island and settle down to bask.

The adults discussed the problem during their midday rest. Normally Po didn't listen to this kind of talk—it was adult stuff—but the crocodile had really scared him and he wanted to know what they were going to do about it.

"Var is right," said Kern. "This crocodile eats all the deer. It eats the swimming birds. They are afraid. They do not come."

The others grunted agreement and sat in gloomy silence.

"We see only one crocodile," said Chogi. "Are there others in this place?"

The men discussed the question among themselves and agreed that there was probably only this one monster in the inlet. Either it had eaten any smaller ones, or it had driven them away.

"Then I say this," said Chogi. "We are weak. We are tired. Bodu must have food. No food, her baby dies. Soon Noli's baby is born—five days, ten, I do not know. Noli must have food. Then she is strong, her baby is strong. Here is food. Here is good water. The crocodile is dangerous, dangerous. But we watch all the time. We see it— it is in one place. We go to another place. It does not catch us. I, Chogi, say this is best."

"Do the men kill the crocodile?" asked Bodu.

"Bodu, this is difficult," said Tun. "The crocodile is strong, strong. It is in the water. We cannot hunt it. Its skin is thick. Our digging sticks do not hurt it."

"Tun, you are right," said Chogi. "You hunt it, then perhaps men die. You are few. This is not good."

Everyone muttered agreement, and they

settled down to discussing the precautions they must take against the crocodile.

———

Soon after they moved on, they reached the head of the inlet. Surprisingly there was no river feeding it, not even a dry riverbed. The water seemed to well up from below. On the far side rose a range of low hills, burned just as dry as everywhere else.

In the afternoon they explored along the farther shore of the inlet, keeping well clear of the water. This meant there were promising-looking areas they couldn't safely reach, but they found enough to eat elsewhere.

That evening, to get away from the insects, they moved up into the hills and found a good place for a camp among some large boulders near a grove of dead trees. They could see down to the inlet, but the main marsh was just out of sight behind a low ridge.

When they settled around their fire, Po didn't sit with Noli and the others. Instead, he found a place where he could hear the men talk, in case they said anything about the crocodile. All day, off and on, he had been thinking about the monster, and remembering the horrible moment when he'd been running away from its charge and had looked back and seen that it was gaining on him. Perhaps, after all, they'd think of a way of killing it. They were strong and brave, especially Suth. Po was sure they could do it, somehow.

But to his disappointment they spent the evening discussing what they'd do with their time until Noli's baby was born. There wasn't anything to hunt here, and the women and children could forage for everyone. So the men decided that in a day or two some of them would explore farther westward along the marsh, while others would head inland to the salt pan Yova had found—less than a day's journey from here, they thought—and bring back fresh supplies of salt.

At least that let Po lie down to sleep that night, happy with the dream he'd had before, about how he would go off alone to the salt pan and bring back the wonderful white salt.

His waking dream turned into his sleeping dream, and that turned into a nightmare, a bad one. He was walking proudly along in the moonlight with a lump of glittering salt, as heavy as he could carry, but then it started to get smaller and dirtier, and the moon set, and there was nothing in his hands, but it was too dark to see where he'd dropped the salt—or put it down, he couldn't remember—but there was something nearby in the dark—he could hear its snorting breath....

He started to run, but his feet were heavy as rocks, and now he could hear and feel the deep thump of that hummocking charge....

He woke with his yell stuck in his throat. The thump was the slamming of his own heart. Every muscle was locked stiff. His arms and legs were like digging sticks. He couldn't move a finger....

Slowly the terror faded. His hands loosened, and then his limbs. Shuddering, he pushed himself up and looked around. There was a half moon high in the west, shining on the dark bodies sleeping quietly among the boulders. Stupid Po. It hadn't been real, just a bad dream. It was all right.

As he was lying down again to try to get back to sleep, somebody stirred. Noli, only a couple of paces away. It was a sudden movement, as if she'd already been lying awake and had heard somebody whisper her name.

She sat straight up and seemed to stare directly at Po. The moon shone full in her face. Her eyes were wide open, but they looked stony and dead in the moonlight.

Slowly she raised an arm, stretched out a finger, and pointed at Po. She spoke, not in her own voice but in a soft, deep whisper, the voice of Moonhawk.

"Kill the crocodile."

Oldtale
Twoheads

Tov journeyed to Tarutu Rock. There he drank at the dewtrap and filled his gourd. Then he went west into the desert, into the Demon Places.

The parrot went with him, perching on his head. All day it slept.

Tov found no water. The sun was behind him, and over him, and shone in his eyes, and his gourd was empty. He came to Twoheads.

Twoheads grew from the desert, as a tree grows, with roots that go deep, deep. He had arms but no legs. The parrot woke and saw him. It left Tov and flew to a rock.

Tov said, "Do you have food? Do you have water? I see none."

Twoheads answered, both mouths speaking together, "We have food. We have water."

Tov said, "I am hungry. I am thirsty. My gourd is empty. Give me food and water."

Twoheads said, "This is our place. We know no other. Our food and our water are beneath us, deep, deep. We do not give. We are Twoheads."

Tov laughed.

Twoheads said, "What is this noise?"

Tov said, "It is laughter. I laugh at your folly. I say in my heart, *See this Twoheads. He has this one place. He knows no other. A stranger comes. He knows many places. He has many tales. Twoheads gives food and water. The stranger tells tales. He speaks of many places. They are happy together, Twoheads and the stranger. They laugh.*"

Twoheads said, "We do not give. We do not laugh. We are Twoheads."

Tov said, "Twoheads, hear me. I make you laugh. Then you give me food and water. I do not make you laugh. I go away. Is this good?"

Twoheads said, "This is good. We do not laugh."

Tov said, "I tell you a tale of folly. There is a man. His name is Tov. He sees a woman. Her name is Gata. She is beautiful, beautiful. He goes to her father. He says, *Give me Gata for my mate*."

Now the parrot flew softly from its rock and perched between the heads of Twoheads. Twoheads did not feel it. Tov continued the tale.

"Gata's father said, *First you bring me a gift. Bring me the tooth of Fododo, the Father of Snakes. Bring me the poison tooth*. Tov answered, *For Gata I do this thing*. Was not this Tov a great fool?"

Now the parrot cried between the heads of Twoheads. Its cry was laughter. It flew away.

The left head turned to the right head. It said, "You laughed."

The right head answered, "It was you."

They were angry. They fought. They bit and struck blows. The left hand struck the right head and the right hand struck the left head.

Their blood flowed. It fell to the ground. Tov ran with his gourd and caught it as it fell. It was yellow, like honey, and sweet. It was food, it was water, as is the juice of stoneweed.

Tov filled his gourd and went on his way. The parrot went with him.

When it grew dark Tov said, "Parrot, this is a place of demons. One must watch all night. All day you slept on my head. Now I sleep and you watch."

He lay down and slept. In the dark the parrot was Falu. All night she watched. Tov woke in the dark. By starlight he saw the shape of one who watched. He said in his heart, *This is Gata*. He called her name.

Falu answered, "Tov, you dream. Gata is far and far. Sleep."

Tov slept. In the morning he woke. Falu was a parrot again.

5

Po lay awake till dawn, miserable with fear. He was more afraid of the crocodile than he'd ever been of anything in his life. Everyone else was afraid of it too, even Tun and Suth, but to them it was just a big, dangerous animal. To Po it was something else. He'd recognized it the moment he'd seen it. The crocodile was a demon. It was the thing in his nightmare, alive and real in the daytime world.

Who could he talk to about it? Who would understand and not just try to comfort him by saying, "Don't be afraid, it isn't a real demon. It's only a nightmare"? Not even Suth, he felt. Noli, perhaps, and he could ask her too what she'd meant when she'd pointed at him like that. Or what Moonhawk had meant. If Noli remembered—she didn't always. Anyway, he'd ask her. At least she wouldn't laugh at him.

But when the others woke and started to get ready for the day, Noli was busy with Tor. Tor was worried about the Porcupines, whom they'd last seen when they'd separated onto opposite sides of the river. How were they doing? Had they also found food and water? If they hadn't, they'd all be dead by now. Because Tor and Noli couldn't talk to each other, they made up for it by spending much more time together than most pairs of mates did, sitting close and hugging and stroking each other. Noli seemed to understand what Tor was thinking, without any words, and she said he understood her the same way. Only it was all far slower than words, and much more to do with feelings and things like that.

Now she was trying to comfort him, and tell him she was sure his friends were all right, so Po settled down a little way off and waited for them to finish. After a while Mana came and sat beside him and offered him a bit of roast blueroot left over from last night. He shook his head.

"Po, you do not eat," she said. "Why is this?"

"I am not hungry," he muttered.

"Po, you are sad," she said. "What is your sadness? Tell."

He sighed, and in a low voice, not looking at her, told her about his dream, and waking. She didn't answer at once, but took his hand in hers and sat thinking. Then, without letting go, she rose to her feet.

"Come," she said. "Now you tell Tinu."

"No," he said, without moving. "I do not want this."

"Come," she repeated firmly. "This is good for Tinu."

She pulled him up. Both reluctant and relieved he followed her to where Tinu was grinding grass seed by spreading it out on a flat boulder and rocking a rounded stone back and forth across it. Since the feast when Chogi had suggested that she and Nar should choose each other for mates, Tinu had been even quieter and more withdrawn than usual. Now she hardly seemed to notice as Po muttered his story again, and when he'd finished she continued rocking the stone back and forth, and sweeping the seeds back together as they spread out, without saying anything.

"Tinu," said Mana. "How do we kill this crocodile?"

Tinu stopped her work and looked directly at Po. For the first time in days he saw her smile her twisted smile.

"Po…this is…difficult," she mumbled. "I think."

Po thanked her, and left her to her seed grinding.

———

Tinu did think, too. Po could tell, because several times while they were foraging down at the inlet he saw her standing by herself, quite still, heedless of the cloud of insects swarming around her and crawling over her body. Then her hands would start to weave invisible shapes in front of her, and she'd frown at them and shake her head and irritably brush the insects away and go back to foraging.

This made Po feel that he didn't need to worry about the problem for himself, so he went off into a good dream in which he, Po, found a secret way across the marsh and led everybody over to the wonderful Good Places on the farther side. Before long he was far away, enjoying the imaginary feast after they'd caught their first deer, and of all the boasts and praises around the fire none was better than Po's, who had found the way across the marsh.

Without warning the ground gave way under his feet. He landed with a bump and shouted aloud with the shock of it. Suth, just ahead of him, turned and laughed.

"Po," he said, "the hunter watches where he puts his foot."

Several other foragers had seen what happened and were laughing too. Nar was one of them. Po scrambled out of the pit he'd dropped into—it was only waist deep—and kicked angrily at the mat of fallen grass stems that had hidden it.

"I watch," he snarled. "See, this grass hides the hole."

Suth laughed again and turned away. Po was still uselessly trying to think of something else to say when Tinu came and kneeled beside the hole.

Carefully she rearranged the grass stems to cover it and then scattered some handfuls of loose dirt over them.

"Tinu, what do you do?" asked Po.

"Po...we kill...crocodile...." she answered. "You show...how."

During the midday rest Po watched her chip out a little circular pit in the ground, and then fiddle with twigs and stems to cover it, and finally hide it under a layer of fine dirt. When she was ready, Po fetched Suth, and Tinu showed him how the crocodile could be lured onto the trap and made to fall through into the pit. She used a stubby twig for the monster and a smaller one for the person who would be the living bait to tempt it out of the water.

"Like we kill the demon lion?" said Suth. And then, smiling, "Po, you are bait again?"

Po scowled. This was a tease he didn't enjoy, because it was about one of his stupid-Po times, so long ago that he didn't remember. But he kept getting told how he'd gone running off into a dangerous place, and Noli had come after him. Then this demon lion had almost caught them, but Noli had run with Po to the trap that the men had built, which meant that someone up above could drop a rock on the lion and kill it.

When Tinu had rebuilt the model, Suth fetched the rest of the men and showed them her idea. They discussed it around the fire that evening, but they weren't very interested.

"This is much, much work," said Kern.

The others laughed, because Kern always avoided serious hard work if he could, but then Var said, "Kern speaks truth. There is food here for five days, six days, I do not know. There is no meat. Soon we must go. Do we make ourselves weak, digging this hole? I say no."

Net said, "I say we fetch salt. Some fetch salt. Some journey west. They look for a new Good Place."

They discussed it to and fro, but decided in the end to spend the next day gathering extra food for the two expeditions to take with them, and then to set out on the day after that. If the group exploring the edge of the marsh came back without finding a fresh source of food, then they would think about trying to kill the crocodile.

That night Po had his nightmare again, just as bad as before, only this time he was by the inlet and the crocodile was coming and cleverly he was running toward the trap the men had dug...but they hadn't, they'd gone to fetch salt instead, and Po was alone, alone in the dark desert, lost, and his legs wouldn't run, and the horrible thud was coming nearer and nearer....

This time when he woke, Noli didn't stir. It was the same again the next night. He was too terrified to get back to sleep, so he crept out of the camp in the dark and made his way up to the ridge, and settled down there to stare out over the marshes.

During the night the heat haze cleared away, and bands of pale mist formed, very beautiful under the setting moon. Then, just as the sun rose, these too cleared, and for a little while he could see the whole marsh, reed beds and mudbanks and water, with fair-sized islands here and there, some of them with real trees on them. Po would have liked to stay and search for signs of a path, but by now the camp was stirring, and he didn't want to answer questions about where he'd been, so he slipped back and joined the others.

He was afraid of the crocodile during the day too, but it was a different kind of fear, the same as everyone else's. They all kept clear of the dangerous places, and stayed far away from the water whenever they couldn't see the monster basking on one of its islands, but most of the time it was no worse than a serious nuisance. Only when the call went up from one of the lookouts to warn everyone that the crocodile had left its island did Po feel a shadow of his night-time fear. Then he would gaze out across the peaceful surface of the inlet and know that the monster was hidden somewhere underneath, almost certainly coming nearer and nearer, trying once more to catch somebody being careless.... That was something like the nightmare.

As soon as the men had set out on their expeditions Chogi called the women together.

"Hear me," she said, in her solemn, anxious manner. "I, Chogi, say this. The men are gone. Now we women dig the pit. The men come back. It is done. The men kill the crocodile. We have meat. We reach more plant food. We stay here ten days, and ten more. Noli's baby is born. It is strong. We are strong. We gather food. We store it. Then we journey on, far and far. Is this good?"

They all agreed and started in as soon as they had found enough food for the day. They chose a spot about twenty paces up from one of the patches of open ground that sloped down to the water, cut themselves digging sticks like the men's, and started to dig.

Meanwhile the older children, Po, Mana and Nar, broke branches off bushes and built a low barrier between the shoreline and the pit, so that they could keep watch without the crocodile being able to see them so dangerously close to the water. When it was ready, they spread out behind it and stared across the still waters of the inlet. Each of them had a pile of rocks beside them, ready to throw.

It wasn't long before Mana called softly and pointed. Po stared. Yes! There! A dark shape like a piece of waterlogged wood just breaking the surface, but moving very gently, closer and closer....

Nar was at that end of the barrier. Mana and Po ran to join him. As soon as the crocodile was in range they stood up and flung their rocks. They'd all been throwing rocks at targets almost since they were babies, because that was one of their vital skills. A good hunter would expect to knock a bird out of a tree at least one time in three if he got a clear shot at it. Now a shower of rocks rained suddenly down around the monster's snout. At least one scored a direct hit. There was a violent swirl in the water beyond, and when the surface settled the crocodile was gone.

Po went back to his place and crouched there with his heart pounding. Time passed, and then he and Mana both saw the same dark patch some way out, again coming slowly shoreward. This time it vanished below the surface before it came in range, but the inlet was so still that Po could see the faint ripple made by something large, moving just below the surface, aiming for his end of the barrier. He called, and the others ran to help. When the ripple was near enough they showered the place with rocks, and again there was that sudden heavy swirl in the water as the crocodile turned and fled.

It tried once more that morning before it gave up and returned to its island. It stayed there, basking, through the hottest part of the afternoon, so Po and Nar went to help carry soil away from the pit, while Mana kept watch alone.

It was heavy work. Tinu had woven mats from reeds. Two of the women loosened the dirt with digging sticks. Four others scooped it out onto mats with their hands, and the rest dragged it clear on the mats. After a while these fell apart, but there were plenty of reeds, so Tinu was kept busy weaving fresh mats. Any rocks they dug out they put aside, the smaller ones for throwing at the crocodile, and the big ones for the men to use later, when they'd caught it.

After a while Mana called to say that the crocodile had left its island, so Po and Nar ran to help drive it away. Four times more that afternoon the enemy came nosing in, each time seeming bolder, getting nearer, and staying longer. The last time, instead of heading back out of range, it turned along the shoreline, as if it were searching for a way past them, while they followed it, yelling and flinging their rocks, until it disappeared beyond the thicket that lay along the water's edge.

By now it was getting dark, and they could no longer keep watch in safety. The diggers were exhausted too, so they gave up and trooped back to their camp. On his way, Po jumped into the pit and found it was already waist deep.

He lay down that night feeling pleased and cheerful. With a little help from Mana and Nar, he, Po, had kept the demon crocodile at bay all day. He'd beaten it. If he could do that once, he could do it again. He could do it in his dreams.

But no. The daytime triumph made no difference to the night horror. He was crouched behind the barrier, watching with the others, but then he was alone, and it was dark, and he was staring out over the moon-lit inlet, waiting for the attack, and the rocks that he'd piled ready were somehow gone, and the monster was already ashore, behind him in the dark...and now the thud of that terrifying charge began....

He woke then as usual, and crept out of the camp and up to his watch point, where he sat staring over the dark marshes, waiting for sunrise.

The next two days were much the same. At some point the children must have scored some good hits on the crocodile, which had hurt it even through its armored hide. At least it seemed warier for a while, turning away as soon as the first rocks splashed down. But it didn't give up.

Meanwhile the women kept digging. The work became harder as the pit got deeper, and by the time the men returned with the salt, on the second afternoon, the sides had to be shored up with branches to stop them from falling in. Half teasingly, the men praised the women, but they didn't stay to help. Their excuse was that on their way back, already laden with salt, they had found a place where there were good cutter stones. The next morning they set out to collect them, leaving the women to work on alone.

On the fourth day there was a change. The crocodile wasn't on its island, and when they reached the inlet they found to their alarm that it had been ashore in the night. The barrier had been pushed aside in two places, and they could see the creature's huge footprints and the dragging groove of its tail all over the area around the pit. They rebuilt the barrier, and Po and Nar crouched tensely down to watch while Mana went to collect more rocks.

Almost at once the crocodile attacked. It came in a single rush, without warning, straight out of the water, lashing the surface to foam and beginning that awful pouncing leap as it burst through the middle of the barrier with the water still streaming from its dark scaly flanks. If Mana had been at her place it would surely have gotten her.

Po had a rock ready in his hand. He yelled and flung it and raced up the slope. The women were helping each other scramble from the pit, and then they were all fleeing from the attack. At the top of the slope they turned and watched the monster snuffling frustratedly around the pit, smelling the traces of the good fresh meat it hungered for.

Po studied it, shuddering. Sometimes, when he was only thinking about it, he wondered if he wasn't making it even bigger in his imaginings than it really was. But he'd been right. It was massive and horrible. He wondered if the pit was going to be big enough to hold it, supposing the men could lure it into falling in. At last it gave up and dragged itself back to the water and disappeared. When they saw it climb out onto the nearest island they went back to work, with one of the children to keep an eye on it.

Twice more that morning it attacked, but it didn't seem to realize that the watcher could see when it left the island, so everyone was safely out of reach by the time it came ashore. The interruptions were maddening, because the women were determined to finish before the men came home that evening. So they worked on through the dense, steamy heat of midday, with the sweat streaming from them and a cloud of insects as thick as the marsh haze swarming around them.

By early afternoon the pit was deep enough and they started to roof it in with reeds, propping them up at the center with twiggy branches. That took a long while. When the sun was more than halfway down the sky, and Po was dragging an armful of cut reeds up the slope, he heard Nar call from the barrier. The crocodile had once again left its island. He dropped the reeds and was moving to safety when Chogi called to him from the pit.

"Po, bring the reeds. Go to watch. Mana go too. Stay far from the water. Almost we finish. You see the crocodile. You shout. You run. We run. Say this to Nar."

So the three watchers took up their posts well above the barrier, to give themselves enough of a start if the crocodile attacked again. Po waited, tense as ever. By now he could judge almost exactly how long it would take the crocodile to cross from the island.... Just a little longer...

"He is there," called Mana, and pointed.

Po saw it at almost the same moment, the slight churning of the still surface, ten and ten paces out, coming faster now....

"Danger!"

All three watchers shouted together. Po was already running. The women were scrambling out of the pit, just ahead of him. He looked to the right. Mana was racing up the slope....

Where was Nar?

He glanced back. Nar was there, running too. But there was something wrong with his leg. The crocodile was already hurtling out of the water, leaping at the barrier, bursting through.... It saw Nar limping ahead and turned toward him. Nar was too slow....

Suddenly his leg got better, and he started to run, not up the slope but slantwise across it, straight into the crocodile's path. The crocodile was almost on him. It hummocked itself up into a final spring.

Nar flung himself violently to his left, almost at the edge of the pit. At once he was back up and running on. Behind him there was a tearing crash as the crocodile landed on the half-finished roof of the pit and tumbled through.

The women yelled and rushed down the slope. As they reached the pit the crocodile reared up out of it, scrabbling with its forelegs for a grip on the rim. Zara struck full force at its head with her digging stick. Yova picked up one of the big rocks they'd laid ready, raised it two-handed over her head, and flung it. The rock thudded into the monster's neck. It bellowed and fell back.

But it was huge. As Po had thought, the pit wasn't really big enough to hold it. Left to itself it could have scrambled out without difficulty, but each time it tried, the women drove it back. Po darted in when he got the chance and flung anything he could find. Then the rim gave way on one side, right under Tinu's feet, but Yova caught her by the arm and hauled her to safety. The monster started to crawl up the slope, but Moru darted forward and struck at it from the side, right in the eye.

It bellowed with pain and rolled away, slithering back into the pit with its great tail lashing uselessly around, finishing half on its side amid the mess of reeds and branches in the bottom. Chogi and Yova were already heaving up a boulder so large that the two of them could barely lift it. Judging their moment they swung it out over the edge and let it fall. It struck the crocodile on the foreleg below the shoulder. There was another bellow of pain. The crocodile thrashed violently and managed to right itself, but the leg was now clearly broken, and when it tried to clamber up the slope it couldn't get a hold and fell back while more rocks rained down on it, until there were none left to throw.

Women and children stood around the pit, panting, and waited for the monster to die. It made a few more feeble efforts to climb out, but at last simply lay and twitched, and then was still.

"We kill the crocodile," said Chogi solemnly. "We women do this."

The men came back in the sunset, both parties together. Po had gone up to the camp to wait for them, and from his watch place he saw them trudging wearily along the rough slope that led down to the marsh.

From the way they walked he could tell that they had found no fresh Good Places.

Happily he ran to meet them and took Suth's hand.

"Do not go to the camp," he said. "Come to the inlet. There is a thing to see."

"What thing, Po?" said Suth, with a tired smile.

"The women finish the pit," guessed Var, who was one of the ones who had seen it half dug.

"No," said Po. "It is more, more. Come."

Suth came, and the others followed. Po raced ahead and shouted from the top of the slope, "The men come! The men come! I do not tell them, *The crocodile is dead!*"

The women had been sitting at the top of the clearing, waving leafy twigs to keep the insects from settling. Now they rose and waited to greet the men, then led them to the pit.

The men gazed down, astounded.

"Chogi, this is good, good," said Tun at last. "Tonight we feast."

By now it was getting dark, but Tun sent Nar to fetch hot embers down from the camp, and they built a small fire and lit twists of dry reed, one after another, to give them enough light to see what they were doing. With a huge effort they dragged the body out of the pit and paced out its length. From snout to tail-tip it was seven good paces.

They cut off a section of the crocodile's tail, which they carried up to the camp and set to roast, while others piled rocks over the rest of the body to keep it safe.

Then they feasted. For the first time in several moons there was meat enough for everyone, and it was wonderful after days of plant stuff.

When they had eaten, Tun rose and held up his hand for silence.

"Hear me," he said. "I, Tun, speak. We men went to the sunset. We went far and far. We found bad places, Demon Places, no food, foul water, marsh water. We come back. We are hungry, we are sad. Fear is in our stomachs.

"We find the women. They say happy words to us. They kill the crocodile. To you, men, I say, *This is a deed of heroes*. Let Chogi speak. Let her make her boast."

Everyone shouted. Chogi rose and held up her hand and waited. She didn't look any different from usual, Po thought, though he'd never heard of a leader inviting one of the women to boast like this.

"Hear me," she said when everyone was silent. "I, Chogi, speak. I speak for the women. I praise all the women. First I praise Tinu. She saw Po fall into a pit. She thought in her heart, *This way we kill the crocodile*. It is Tinu's thought. She is clever. Next I praise the women. I praise Yova, Zara, Dipu, Galo, Bodu, Runa, Moru, Noli, Shuja. We dug the pit. The work was hard, hard. I praise Tinu again. She made clever mats. The women carried dirt, much and much. I praise the children who watched for the crocodile. They watched well. They threw rocks. They drove it away. I praise the boy Nar. Nar was clever. He was brave. The crocodile came from the water. We ran. We ran fast. Nar ran. He ran slow. He ran like a boy with a hurt leg. The crocodile sees him. It says in its heart, *This boy's leg is hurt. I catch him*. Nar runs to the pit. The crocodile is close, close. Nar jumps to the side. The crocodile does not see the pit. It falls in the pit.

"We women come. We fight the crocodile. We strike it with digging sticks. We hurl great rocks...."

Po had stopped listening. He felt his heart would burst with shame and anger. He could have borne it, perhaps, if Chogi had just named and praised Nar, but why did she have to name Po too, not for anything clever or brave he'd done, but only reminding everyone about that stupid business of falling into that hole? And she hadn't even bothered to name him for the scrap of praise she'd given him. He was just one of the children who'd kept lookout and driven the crocodile off with rocks. Po was certain some of his rocks hadn't only scored hits— they'd actually hurt the monster, and scared it from attacking more in those first three days. *And* he'd helped in the fight around the pit.... But all anyone was going to remember about his part in the adventure would be that he'd fallen into a stupid hole! And Tinu wouldn't even have been thinking about killing the crocodile if Po hadn't asked her to....

And then, worse still, they let Nar stand up and make a separate boast of his own, and he did it well, not stammering or tongue-tied, as Po had been when he'd accidentally driven off the lioness and saved Kern's life, but choosing good words and saying them easily.

Po lay down to sleep still hurt, still furious. Strangely, his nightmare didn't return, but he woke in the early dawn with two thoughts fixed in his mind. Somehow he, Po, was going to find a way across the marshes. And when he'd done that he was going to find a mate for Tinu. To prove to himself that he really meant it, when no one was looking he stole a small lump of the new salt and put it in his gourd, so that he would have it handy to give to Tinu and the man, whoever he was, when they chose each other.

Oldtale

Bagworm

Tov journeyed west. The parrot went with him, the little gray parrot with the yellow tail feathers. All day it perched on his head and slept. The sun was behind him and over him and shone in his eyes, and his gourd was empty. He came to the place of Bagworm.

Bagworm lay in the desert. He was a great worm, and his belly was a bag. It was full of water. He put his ear to the ground, and heard footsteps. He said in his heart, *One comes. He finds no water. He dies. I eat him.*

He spewed his water onto the

ground and crept away. Tov saw the water and ran toward it. Bagworm sucked with his mouth, and the water returned to his belly and was gone.

Again Tov saw water, and ran, and the water was not there. He said in his heart, *This is magic stuff. But I am Tov.*

A third time he saw water, but he did not run. He said, "Wake, little parrot. Fly high. See the water. Soon it goes. Follow it."

The parrot flew high. Then Tov ran. Bagworm heard him and sucked with his mouth and drew the water to him. The parrot followed.

Now Tov went softly, following the parrot, until he came to the place where Bagworm lay. Tov came on him from behind, and leaped into the air, and landed on the great fatness of his belly, so that all the water spewed out.

Then Tov caught Bagworm by the throat and crammed his mouth with dirt. With the butt of his digging stick he rammed it firm. Now Bagworm could not suck the water into himself.

Tov drank, and filled his gourd. He saw creatures in the water, whose name is fish.

They are people food. He took them, and journeyed west.

At nightfall he camped, and ate fish until his belly was full. The parrot did not eat. Fish are not parrot food.

Tov said, "Little parrot, I am weary. All day you slept on my head. Now keep watch while I sleep."

Tov slept. The parrot perched on a rock at his feet. In the dark she became Falu. She was hungry and ate the fish, spitting out the bones. Then she kept watch.

Tov woke. By the light of the stars he saw Falu, where she sat on the rock at his feet. He called, "Gata?"

Falu answered, "It is not Gata. She is far and far. Tov, you dream. Now sleep."

Tov slept. When it was day, he woke and saw the parrot, where it perched on the rock at his feet. Beside the rock he saw the bones of fish.

He said in his heart, *I do not dream these bones. This parrot is clever, clever. But I am Tov.*

6

The next morning, with great difficulty, the men cut the head off the crocodile, and set it on a pole beside the camp, to show what the women had done. Now that the monster was dead, they could safely harvest far more of the inlet, wading into the water if they needed to reach parts of the dense thickets that grew along the shoreline. And there was enough crocodile meat for several days, though it started to go bad almost at once in the steamy heat. But their stomachs were strong, and even when it truly stank they ate it without falling ill.

The extra food meant that now they could stay until Noli's baby was born, so they settled down to wait.

Soon Po was very restless. If he got the chance, he would sneak off down to the shoreline, looking for places where the mud seemed drier and firmer than elsewhere. Once he ventured out a few paces onto a dried mudbank, but then it got softer, and he remembered how suddenly Net had fallen through and just barely been dragged out, so, shuddering with fear, he edged his way back to safety.

But he found other patches where flattened tangles of reeds had fallen across the mud, and here the stems seemed to spread his weight so that he could walk with confidence. These patches didn't lead anywhere, of course, but suppose he cut a whole lot of reeds and laid them down as he went....

He was thinking about that one evening when he remembered the mats that Tinu had woven to carry the dirt away when the women were digging the crocodile trap. The next day he went and found several of them still by the pit, not too battered. At his next chance he took them along to the main marsh and tried them out. They didn't feel safe only one layer thick, so he laid them down double, making a path three mats long, and carefully crawled onto it.

When he reached the end he realized that he could now drag the first pair of mats around and lay them down in front of him, and so move one mat farther. And again. And again.

He was ten and more paces out onto the mud before he lost his nerve and turned around and worked his way back until he could stand, quivering with relief, on solid ground and wipe the worst of the mud off his arms and legs.

I walk in the marsh, he thought as he sneaked back to join the others. *I, Po, find the way. But it is slow, slow.*

Suth noticed his return.

"Po, where do you go?" he asked.

"Suth, it is secret," Po answered.

Suth smiled. Po guessed what he was thinking—*Boy stuff. Boys are full of their small secrets*. But this wasn't a small secret. It was big, big. Po decided he wasn't going to tell anyone about it until he had actually reached the first island, a little west of the inlet.

For that he needed more mats. It was far too slow crawling along with only three pairs of mats. If he had five pairs he could lay down a longer path and move three pairs at a time. That would be much faster.

When the men weren't foraging, they were making fresh cutters with the rocks they'd brought back. Kern was teaching Nar how to do it, but Po's hands weren't strong enough yet, so he'd asked Suth to make him a small cutter of his own. It was a good one, with an edge both sharp and strong, which would last some while before it blunted. No one thought there was anything unusual about Po wanting to try it out—all boys were like that with cutters—and the obvious thing was for him to go off on his own and cut a few reeds, so it was easy for him to get away and carry on with his plan.

But making mats was much trickier than he'd guessed. Po copied Tinu's as carefully as he could, but his weren't nearly as good. It took him all his spare time in two days to make another pair, and he then decided that would have to be enough. On the third day he collected the eight mats and started off on his adventure. He was scared now, both of the danger and of what Suth would say about it, but he wasn't going to give up.

He had studied the island he was aiming for from his lookout above the camp, just after sunrise when the mists had cleared and before the haze hid the marshes again. It wasn't all that far from the shore across a level stretch of mud. And it had real trees on it.

So he didn't follow the shoreline, but went some distance up along the slope, because from there he could see the treetops poking above the haze. As he came opposite them and was about to start down to the marsh, a little swirling dust storm came scurrying out of the hills, straight toward him. Just in time he flung his mats on the ground and kneeled on them so that they wouldn't be carried away, and then crouched with his hands over his face while a hail of grit and twigs, caught up by the flurry, slashed against his skin.

In a few moments it was gone, and he rose and watched it whirl crazily down the slope and out into the marsh, tearing the haze apart and leaving a clear patch, which moved across the mudbank, dying as it went. It vanished just as it reached the island, so Po caught only a glimpse of its eastern tip. But in that glimpse he saw a man.

The man was standing on one leg, at the edge of the water, still as a heron. His other leg was bent, with the sole of that foot resting against the straight knee. His right arm was raised to his shoulder, holding a long, slim stick. His head was bent, peering at the water. Po understood at once that he was doing what herons do. He was fishing.

Then the haze closed up and hid him.

Of course Po knew what he ought to do. He should run at once and tell Suth and Tun what he had seen. But he wasn't going to. He told himself the man was there now. By the time he'd reached the others and brought them back, the man might be gone. And there were only eight mats. They wouldn't be strong enough to carry the weight of a grown man. But if Po could reach the island and watch this stranger, without himself being seen, and perhaps follow him when he left...

Why?

Because the man must have got to the island somehow. That meant he knew a way across the marshes!

Before he could change his mind, Po ran down to the shore, chose a place and laid the first pair of mats on the mud. He crawled onto them, reached back for the next pair, and then the next, and the next. Only when he'd crawled back to fetch the first two pairs, and so cut himself off from firm ground, did he hesitate, biting his lip. It still wasn't too late to go and fetch Suth.

No. He, Po, was going to do this thing.

So he set off, working as he had the day before, moving his little path steadily out across the mud. Soon he was in a rhythm. The surface was caked hard, and he could barely feel it move when he crawled forward onto the next pair of mats. Now he could see the island, a vague brownish mass in the dense haze. And looking back he could no longer see the shore. He must be halfway there, at least.

Then the surface changed, becoming softer and stickier. His mats became clogged with mud, and when he dragged them forward they started to fall apart from their own weight. He did his best to be careful, but each time he moved one it became looser, and pieces fell away. The two he had made himself were useless almost at once....

He looked back, and saw nothing but mud and the sticky ooze he had crossed. He looked ahead, and the reedbed that lined the island seemed very near. He could see the individual stems. He would have to get there. His mats wouldn't last long enough to get him back to the shore. Perhaps he could make himself fresh ones on the island.

For the last few paces he abandoned the ruined mats and lay on his belly and squirmed his way forward over the stinking, clinging ooze, until he could haul himself onto a layer of fallen reed stems.

With intense relief he stood and walked carefully along beside the dense tangle of growing reeds, looking for an opening. But after a little while the mudbank ended at a patch of open water, so he was forced to turn back. He chose a place where the tangle didn't look quite as hopeless as elsewhere and started to wrestle his way through the reedbed.

It was horrible. Soon he could scarcely move. With a great effort he would force his way through a gap, find himself trapped, struggle on a little farther, and be trapped again. The sweat streamed down. Swarms of insects, disturbed by his efforts, gathered eagerly around him. He could no longer tell which way he was heading. He felt helpless, desperate, terrified, utterly alone. Even if he got free of the reeds, he'd never get back across the mud. The others would never find where he was. He was going to die, caught in this horrible place, this Demon Place—stupid, stupid Po.

To his shame he started to sob. His breath as he dragged it in moaned in his throat. His tears blinded him. He groped forward.

And something caught him by the wrist.

He yelped with the shock of it, and in the next instant realized that the thing was a hand. It dragged him forward and flung him down on a patch of clear ground. He heard a hiss like the hiss of an angry snake and looked up, raising his arm against the expected blow.

Through the blur of his tears he saw a face. It was the face of a demon.

His mouth wrenched itself open, but the scream jammed in his throat. The face was the shape of a man's face, but striped bright yellow, like the tail of a parrot, and with purple blotches around the eyes.

The demon snorted. Po cringed, and then some corner of his mind that hadn't frozen with terror recognized the sound. It was almost the same snort that Tor used when he was surprised or puzzled by something new to him. Tor didn't have words. He couldn't say "What is this?" Instead, he snorted.

Po's voice came back to him.

"I...I...I...Po..."

All he could think of was to offer the demon a gift. He knew that in the old days, when a Kin came to a Good Place that belonged to some other Kin, this was what they used to do. He scrabbled in his gourd and found a hard lump. Yes, the bit of salt he'd stolen. Salt was a real gift. He cupped it in his hands and offered it to the demon.

The demon snorted again, with surprise and took it. The hand didn't have great, hooked talons, like a demon's in the Oldtales, but ordinary fingers, people fingers. There was a yellow circle on the back of it, but seeing it up close Po realized that wasn't the color of the skin. It was some sort of yellow stuff that had been smeared on. The skin itself was brown, not as dark as Po's but like Tor's skin.

The demon was a man. He had colored stuff smeared onto him to make him look like a demon.

With a gasp of relief Po watched the man raise the salt to his mouth and lick it, and then grunt. Again Po recognized the sound. It wasn't the same, but it was something like the grunt Tor used to mean he was pleased.

Feeling much better, Po rose to his feet

and stood while he and the man looked at each other. Now that he wasn't stupid with terror Po saw that the man could easily have been one of Tor's people, the Porcupines. He was taller and skinnier than Tor himself, but he had the same thin face and sharp, hooked nose and protruding teeth. After a while he looked at the lump of salt in his palm and offered it back to Po with a questioning grunt, as if he wasn't sure Po meant him to keep it.

Feeling steadily more confident, Po raised both hands, palms forward, fingers spread, and moved them toward the man. At the same time he made a brief double hum in his throat, the second part lower than the first. This was more Porcupine stuff. The Porcupines were always giving each other small gifts. It was one of the things they did instead of talking. Po had once seen three of them passing the same colored pebble to and fro all through a rest time, and then when they'd moved on they'd left it behind. It had been the giving that had mattered, not the gift.

The man made his pleased sound again, even louder. He was wearing what looked like a strip of reed leaf around his waist.

From it dangled several short wooden tubes, not any kind of wood Po knew but more like very thick reed stems. Some of them were stoppered with a wad of leaf. The man opened one, dropped the salt into it, and stoppered it up. He picked up his long stick and turned, gesturing to Po to follow him, then led the way along the narrow path on which they'd been standing.

It came out on the open space at the tip of the island, where Po had first glimpsed the man. Here he kneeled and moved some fallen reeds aside, revealing three fish. He chose one, bit a chunk from its back, took the morsel out of his mouth and offered it to Po.

Po knew about fish. There'd been some in the river that ran through the New Good Places. The Porcupines had sometimes managed to catch one in their bare hands, but the Kin hadn't bothered until the river started to dry up and they found them stranded in pools. Po made the *I thank* noise and chewed the mouthful up. It was very good.

The man went back to what he'd been doing before, standing one-legged, motionless, right at the tip of the island, staring at the water.

Po waited. An insect settled on his neck and bit. He slapped it, and instantly the man turned his head and hissed for silence, then returned to his fishing. Po moved back along the path as far as he could without losing sight of him, picked up a broken piece of reed to use as a swat, and waited again.

Time passed. The man seemed not to move a muscle, not even to breathe. *This is good hunting*, thought Po. There was a saying among the Kin: *The hunter is strong—good. The hunter is swift—better. The hunter is still—best.* People were always telling Po that because he wasn't very good at stillness.

But now he did his very best to be almost as still as the man. It wasn't just that he didn't want to be left alone on this horrible island, with no way back to the Kin. But also, having come this far, having started to make friends, Po wasn't going to give up easily. The man had to know the way across the marshes. There would never be a better chance of finding it.

The stillness ended in a movement as

sudden and sharp as the strike of a snake. The left arm shot out. The bent leg straightened into a huge stride. The body flung forward, with the right arm hurling the long stick ahead of it, out and down, in a thrust that lanced it cleanly into the water. An instant later the man splashed in behind it and disappeared under the foam.

He came up a moment later, grasping a fish in both hands. Po had never seen one as large. It was as long as his arm, with a gaping jaw and thin, curving teeth. The man's stick was still in it, piercing it through, but it was alive and thrashing around in the water while the man fought to hold it. Somehow he shifted his grip and got both hands on his stick, one on each side of the fish's body, and then dragged it to the bank and heaved it ashore. Po ran and caught it by the tail and hauled it clear of the water while the man climbed out. Laughing with triumph the man put his foot close behind the head, pulled the stick out, and stabbed down, piercing the fish through again but this time pinning it to the ground. It lay there, flopping and gasping, and at last was still.

While they waited for it to die, Po looked

at the stick. It was taller than the man, about as thick as Po's thumb and very straight but with knobby rings at intervals along it. He thought it must be another kind of reed. What impressed him was how sharp it must be, to pierce clean through a big fish like that, and how good for throwing. It was lucky the man hadn't thought Po was some kind of animal while he was struggling among the reeds, making all that noise. He could easily have thrown his stick at the sound. Or perhaps Po had been lucky to be weeping aloud, making the sort of noise that only people make.

It looked as if the man thought he'd now done enough hunting for the day. As soon as the fish was dead, he picked it up with his stick still through it, then threaded the three smaller fish onto the point. He lifted the stick and its load onto his shoulder, nodded to Po, and made a double grunt. Again it was a bit different from the Porcupines', but close enough for Po to realize it meant both *I go* and *Good-bye*.

"I come too," said Po firmly. He had no intention of being left behind.

The man looked puzzled, but Po didn't waste time trying to explain what he meant with signs. Knowing Tor and the Porcupines so well, he realized that this wasn't the sort of thing he could get across to this man.

"Tor is not like Tinu," Noli had once explained. "Tinu's mouth is hurt. It cannot make good words. But Tinu has words in her head. Tor does not have words in his head. There is no place for them. I make signs with my hands. These signs are hand words. You understand my signs. For you it is easy. For Tor it is hard, hard."

So now Po guessed it would be no use tapping his own chest and then pointing across the marshes to say, *I want you to take me over there*. Instead he simply grasped the man's free hand and started off along the path. The man still looked puzzled, but he came. The path wasn't wide enough for two, so Po let go of the man's hand, waited for him to pass, and then followed him. The man looked back, shrugged, and walked on.

Oldtale

Stonejaw

Tov journeyed west. The parrot sat on his head, and slept. The sun was behind him, and over him, and shone in his face, and his gourd was empty. He came to the place of Stonejaw.

There he saw a great rock. That was the head of Stonejaw. There was no body, no arms, no legs, only the head. In the rock was a cave. That was the mouth of Stonejaw. Out of it came his song.

> Come into my cave.
> In it is water.
> Hear the sweet water.
> It is cool, cool.

The song was magic. When Tov heard it he forgot the skills of the hunter. He ran to the cave, not looking, not seeing.

The parrot woke and screeched in Tov's ear, so that he could not hear Stonejaw's song. Now he looked and saw. He said in his heart, *This is Stonejaw. The cave is his mouth.*

Beside the cave Tov saw a great rock. He rolled it into the mouth of the cave, between the jaws of Stonejaw. Then he walked through.

The jaws closed on the rock, but could not close further. Tov went to the water and drank, and filled his gourd. Beside the water he saw a dead gazelle, a gazelle of the desert. Stonejaw had caught it. Tov took it and carried it out of the cave.

He said, "Come, little parrot. We have food, we have water. Stonejaw, farewell."

Tov camped, and ate of the gazelle. The parrot did not eat. Gazelle are not parrot food.

Tov said, "Little parrot, all day you slept on my head. Now I sleep. You watch."

When he lay down he put a sharp thorn beneath his ribs. He did not sleep.

In the dark the parrot became Falu. She was hungry, and ate of the gazelle, sucking the marrow from the bones. The noise was loud. Tov heard it, and opened his eyes, and saw her where she sat sucking the marrow bone. He crept softly toward her and caught her by the wrist.

Falu cried aloud. She said, "Tov, let me go."

Tov said, "I do not let you go. Soon it is morning. I see who you are."

Falu wept. She said, "Tov, do not do this. You hold me, you see me. Then your parrot dies, the little gray parrot with the yellow tail feathers."

Tov said in his heart, *I cannot do this. I need my little parrot. She is clever, clever.*

He let go of Falu's wrist, and lay down and slept. In the morning Falu was a parrot again.

7

The path came out on the far side of the island. Looking past the man, Po could see a stretch of mud, and beyond it another island. The man stepped confidently onto the mud and at once started to sink. The mud closed over his foot, but then he stopped sinking and took another pace, and another, checking his foothold each time before he moved on.

Po followed him, stepping exactly in his footprints, and found that there was something solid just below the surface. Curious, he stopped after a while, balanced on one leg, and carefully felt down with his other foot beside the line of footprints. There was nothing there, and nothing on the other side, only this single narrow path.

He bent and probed through the mud with his fingers and felt around. The solid stuff seemed to be a thick layer of reeds, laid all in the same direction. That couldn't have happened by accident. He realized that the reeds must have been put here.

He hurried after the man, before the mud could close over the footprints. Looking back he saw that it had already done so where they'd started from the first island. So if you didn't know exactly where the path was, you couldn't use it.

On the far side of the next island there was a more open shoreline. Some way along it two women were fishing, using sticks like the man's. The man called to them. They turned, stared for a moment, and came running.

The man showed them the fish he'd caught, and they clapped their hands and made the chortling *wo-wo-wo-wo* that Tor used when he wanted to praise someone. They hugged him and fawned on him and stroked him, while he laughed with triumph. Their faces weren't colored like the man's, but they wore the same sort of belt that he did, with the wooden tubes on it. One of them had a baby inside her. Po guessed she must be the man's mate, but he was puzzled by the other one, because she was behaving in exactly the same way. She looked a bit younger than Noli, but he didn't think the man was old enough to be her father.

When they'd finished letting the man know how wonderful he was they turned and stared at Po, making sounds of astonishment. They bent and sniffed him and poked him, and the younger one licked his skin and then rubbed hard at the place with her fingers, while he tried to squirm free. The other two watched, laughing, until she realized that Po's skin color wouldn't come off, and gave up.

They set off together in single file, winding from island to island, mostly using the hidden paths across the mudbanks but sometimes wading through water up to their waists. After a while they came to another of these open channels, and Po saw a group of people standing on the shore of the next island. The three Po was with stopped and squatted to watch, making quiet mutters of excitement, though as far as he could see the other group weren't doing anything special. Then he noticed that one of the men was hunkered down, holding one end of a fishing stick with its other end beneath the water, and jiggling it gently to and fro.

Nothing happened for a while. The usual horrible insects gathered and settled and stung. Po switched at them with a piece of reed. The marshpeople didn't seem bothered by them. The air was dense and hot and steamy. He couldn't see the sun, but it must be high overhead. The Kin would be having their midday rest. No, they'd have noticed by now that Po was missing. They'd be angry and worried and unhappy, and they'd be looking for him despite the heat. They'd find the trail he'd left with his mats on the dried mud near the shore. Perhaps they'd see the bits of broken mat far out across the marsh. They'd think he'd sunk in the mud out there and drowned. *Stupid, stupid Po*, they'd say. He said it now to himself. *Stupid, stupid Po.* Why hadn't he run and told Suth about seeing the man on the island? He started to feel very miserable and alone and far away from his friends.

Now the man he was with picked up the big fish and began to chew at its back. He had trouble getting started, because he couldn't get his mouth around it, so Po felt in his gourd and offered him his cutter. It was already a bit blunt, after cutting all those reeds for the mats, but there were still some sharp places on its edge. The man frowned at it, puzzled, until Po kneeled by the fish and sliced a chunk out and gave it to him, then did the same for each of the women. Though he didn't feel hungry he cut a small piece for himself. The man took the cutter and felt its edge with his thumb, grunted approvingly, and handed it back.

Then he opened one of his belt tubes, took out the lump of salt Po had given him, and crumbled a few crystals onto his piece of fish. Immediately the women started wheedling for some for themselves, and he very grudgingly broke them off a few grains each, but when they begged for more he snorted crossly and shook his head.

Po groped again in the bottom of his gourd and found several crystals that had fallen off the main chunk, so he scraped them out and gave them to the women, who crowed with delight over them.

Suddenly there was a shout from the other bank. Po's three guides were on their feet, jumping with excitement. He ran to look. The man with the stick was standing up now, straining back to stop himself from being pulled into the water. A couple of others were helping. Several more had jumped in. There was a flurry of splashing, and glistening arms and bodies heaving about as they struggled with something below the surface. The stick came loose, and the three holding it tumbled on their backs. The ones in the water were lifting a large creature out, working all together as it thrashed around, and now Po could see that it was a crocodile, a small one, not much longer than his own body. Despite that, it took six people to hold it, one to each leg, one to the tail, and one to grip the jaw and hold it shut.

They hauled it onto the bank and pinned it down while one of the men stabbed it again and again through the eye sockets until it was dead.

Now Po's party picked up their fish and waded into the channel and crossed, splashing the water around and shrieking and yodeling as they went. Po was pretty scared. He guessed this must be a bad crocodile area. None of the Kin would have dreamed of wading into water like this. But he wasn't going to be left behind, so he followed, keeping as close as he could and shrieking and splashing like the others, and climbed out onto the far bank with a sigh of relief.

Everyone gathered around the dead crocodile. They were mostly men, all with differently colored faces, and a few women, who were hugging and stroking some of the men, and making *Praise* noises to them. The man who seemed to be the chief hunter was standing proudly with his foot on the crocodile, and he had three women to himself, while others had none.

Po stared at the scene, bewildered. And then an extraordinary thought came to him. Perhaps these men had more than one mate each. His friend had two, and this chief hunter had three. Which must mean that some of the other men had none at all! Po couldn't imagine how anyone could live like that. It was so weird.

At first the new people were too excited by their catch to notice him, but when they did they weren't friendly. They made their sounds of surprise, and some of them prodded and rubbed his skin, but they snatched at him when they wanted to look at him and shoved him roughly away when they were done.

Then one man tried to grab Po before another had finished with him and neither of them would let go. He yelled as he was pulled to and fro, until the man he'd first met joined in and there was the sort of snarling match he'd often seen among the Porcupines, because they didn't have words to argue with. In the middle of it one of the men gave a sudden jerk and got Po to himself, but then just flung him aside while he went on with the snarling match.

Po crashed into someone's legs and fell, half stunned. As he struggled up, determined not to let anyone see the tears that were starting to come, a hand took his arm and pulled him, much more gently, away from the men. It was the younger of the two women he'd come with. She patted him comfortingly and pushed him behind her until the spat was over.

When the man joined them, she and the other woman stroked him and cooed at him, as if he'd done something almost as wonderful as catching the big fish, and then they left the hunting party to their celebrations and moved on.

Soon the journey became easier. The hidden paths across the mudbanks were firmer, and nearer the surface, and the trails through the reedbeds and islands were wider. From time to time Po saw people fishing from different islands, both men and women, standing in that one-legged heron pose, waiting in total stillness. Though he could see that what they were doing was a kind of hunting, it seemed very different from the sort of hunting he was used to. His sense of loneliness deepened. He didn't understand these marshpeople at all. He felt as helpless as a baby in their world.

And he was completely lost, more lost than he'd ever been in his life, among the shapeless tangle of reedbeds and islands, and with no way of knowing where the sun was, above the dense haze. At last they came to somewhere different, a much larger patch of open water with a cluster of small islands in the middle of it, just mounds rising above the water, almost bare of reeds or trees, with people moving about on them.

Po couldn't see any way across to the islands, but the man led them around the edge of the water until they came to what looked like a long, narrow mudbank running out from the reedbeds to the nearest island, with a reed path laid along the top.

As they approached the place Po's guides each scooped up a handful of mud, and then as they crossed to the island they chose a spot and put the mud down and carefully stamped it in to strengthen the path.

These people were clever, Po thought. They didn't have words or know about cutters, but they knew a lot of things that the Kin didn't know. They must have built the hidden paths through the marshes and chosen these islands for their lair and made them safe for themselves.

Where the path reached the first island, there was a strange, low wall, with a gap in the middle, and a row of poles behind it with objects on top of them. As he came nearer, Po saw that these were crocodile heads—and then, with a thud of the heart, that the whole wall was also made of crocodile heads. Some of them were so old that the flesh and hide had fallen away, leaving only the grinning white skulls. None of them was half as big as the monster that the Kin had killed, but there were tens and tens and tens of them.

Po found them really scary. They gave the entrance the look of a demon place. But the man simply halted at the gap, touched the snout of the largest skull with his hand and led the way on. The women followed without any fuss, so Po did the same.

There were several women and a lot of children on the island, who the moment they saw Po cried out and came crowding around, sniffing and touching him and muttering with surprise. Then a man came striding through, pushing them roughly aside. His face too was colored like a demon's. He stared at Po, snorted with anger, grabbed him by the shoulder, and flung him back toward the entrance.

Immediately a ferocious snarling match began between the two men, but as Po picked himself up he could at once see who was going to win it. This new man was older and more important than Po's guide, who was already backing away from him when the two women took Po by the arms and hustled him down to the water and along the edge of the island to another path. This led to a smaller island which they crossed, again going around by the edge, and so on, past two more islands, till they reached one right at the outside of the group, where they let go of him and put their burdens down. Po guessed that this must be their home. A few moments later the man arrived, looking both anxious and angry.

The three marshpeople did their usual petting and stroking as they settled down, and then the man laid his fish on the ground and pointed at Po's gourd and made a *Give* sound. Guessing what he meant, Po took out his cutter and handed it across. Awkwardly, because he wasn't used to the tool, the man hacked off pieces of fish for everyone. Scraping in the bottom of his gourd, Po found enough crumbs of salt for himself and the two women.

The whole surface of the island was littered with scraps and splinters of reed, and when they'd had enough to eat, the women scooped a hollow in the litter, laid what was left of the fish in it, and covered it over. The man settled down to sharpening his fishing stick by rubbing it with a short piece of pole dipped in gritty mud. The women made storage tubes from pieces of reed, using their teeth to nibble the splintered ends clean. All three seemed jumpy and kept glancing anxiously toward the large island by the entrance path.

After a while Po heard rhythmic shouts floating across the water, mixed in with a strange rattling noise a bit like a lot of woodpeckers tapping on a hollow tree. The three marshpeople jumped up and stared. Po followed their gaze and saw a procession winding its way through the reedbeds on the far side. The man took Po by the shoulders and gave him a firm push to tell him to stay where he was, and then he and the two women hurried off toward the entrance.

Po waited and watched. The procession was mostly hidden by reeds until it reached the path across the water. Then he saw that the men at the front were marching close together in single file with something held at arm's length above their heads. It was the body of the crocodile they had caught. People were running out onto the path to meet it, and then dancing back in front of it. The rattling sound increased, but Po still couldn't see how it was made. Killing a crocodile must be a big thing among these people, he realized. He wished he could have shown them the monster that the Kin had killed.

He waited for a long time, until the gray haze started to turn to gold, and he realized that soon it would be sunset. The color was deeper on the side away from the entrance, so he reckoned that had to be west. He settled down with his chin on his knees and watched the slow change. It filled him with sadness. Though he seemed for the moment to be in a place of safety, he felt very, very lonely. This was the time of day when the weary foragers and hunters would be coming home to their lair and roasting the meat they had caught, and pounding roots and seeds. Then they would eat, with the fire-light flickering on their dark faces, and their eyes glinting with reflected sparks, and talk and tease and boast—Po's people in Po's world, a world he understood, his home. Not this dense, steaming marsh, these strangers with their uncomfortable customs...

New shouts, different, angry.

Coming nearer.

He rose and turned, and saw the two women running across the nearest island, followed by their man. Close behind them came several more men, yelling furiously. The women dashed across the connecting path, but the man stopped when he was halfway over, and turned and faced the attackers. He had no weapons, but he stood in a fighting pose with his hair all bushed out and bellowed at them.

Po watched, terrified. This had to be something to do with him. Now that the men were back from the crocodile hunt, their leader had brought them to get Po. They didn't want this strange child in their place. They were going to kill him, or else throw him off their islands, out into the dreadful marshes, alone in the night. That would be almost as bad.

They halted, yelling, on the shore. Their leader pushed through onto the path and confronted Po's host. Po expected him to back down, as he'd done when the same thing had happened on the main island, but he stood his ground, snarling. *This is my island*, he seemed to be saying. *On it I am leader, not you*. The women watched, murmuring anxiously. The older one grabbed Po's arm and pulled him behind her, where he couldn't be seen.

After a little while the other man snorted and turned away, and the attackers moved off, growling. Po's host strutted back onto the island and the women petted and praised him, but he stood frowning at Po, until Po kneeled in front of him and rapped his knuckles together, three times, as he'd have done if he'd been asking a favor of his own leader, Tun.

"I, Po, thank," he said. "Also I, Po, ask. Tomorrow I go. You show me the path."

He twisted and pointed south, to show what he meant. The man grunted uncertainly but rumpled Po's hair for a moment, and Po felt he was trying to tell him he would look after him if he could.

By now it was almost dark. The women scooped a large hollow in the reed litter, and the three marshpeople settled into it, lying close together with the man in the middle. Po made himself a hollow of his own and lay down in that strange and frightening place, longing with everything that was in him to be away from there, lying among his own people, close to the good red embers of their fire. He wept quietly in the dark, and fell asleep still weeping.

He was shaken awake and had no idea where he was. His left side was covered with insect bites. A woman's voice grunted softly, and he remembered. He sat up and looked around.

It was dark still. The heat haze was gone, and the familiar stars overhead shone almost clear. To the east the sky was faintly gray. Now the woman, softly again, made her *Come* sound. Po rose, groped for his gourd, and slung it over his shoulder. He followed the other three down to the path and across to the first island. They worked their way around it, paddling at the very edge of the water, and so on to the main entrance, never setting foot on anyone else's island. By the time they reached the reedbeds it was almost light. Po saw that the younger woman was carrying the half-eaten fish.

The man led the way in silence, not stopping till they had crossed several more islands. Then they paused only long enough to hack off four portions of fish, and moved on, chewing as they went. As the sun rose, the heat haze formed, and soon Po lost all sense of direction once more. All this time the man had barely looked at him, and Po began to have a sick feeling that he was just being taken away into the marshes to be gotten rid of, and then he'd be left to find his own way home. But the women stayed friendly, especially the younger one, and after a while he recognized the place where the crocodile had been killed, so he started to feel much better. He was going home.

More mud flats, islands, reedbeds, water crossings. And then, on yet another path across yet another island, the man stopped. All three of Po's guides turned and looked at him. The man grunted, *All right?* Po frowned and looked around, and saw that this was the place where the man had first met him, fighting his way through the reeds.

But how was he going to get off the island, across that last dreadful stretch of mud? Perhaps the man knew a way.

Come, he grunted, doing his best to imitate the way the marshpeople made the sound. He led them along the path to the tip of the island where the man had been fishing. The haze wasn't yet quite thick enough to hide the solid land where he'd set out. Po pointed at it and made the light, anxious-sounding moan that meant, *I beg.*

The man frowned, snorted uncertainly, and turned back along the path. Halfway down it he stopped and studied the reeds on his left, shook his head, moved on a little further, grunted, and pushed his way in. As he followed the others, Po realized that they must be using an old path, now partly overgrown, but still nothing like the impossible tangle of reeds to either side.

They came out directly opposite the land, with only a few tens of paces of mud still to cross. The man prodded around with the butt of his fishing stick, nodded, and stepped out onto the mud. He sank deeper in than usual, halfway up his shin, but then found solid footing. He took a couple of paces more, but this time the women didn't follow him, and he turned and came back. Once more all three of them looked at Po. This was an old hidden path across the mud, they seemed to be telling him. If he was careful he should be able to use it on his own. The man took his shoulder and gave him a push toward it.

Po grunted, *I thank*, and felt in his gourd for a gift. He had nothing left except his cutter, so a bit reluctantly he offered it to the man, who took it without hesitation, obviously pleased. The women were watching, waiting. They didn't seem to expect anything, but Po felt strongly that he ought to give them something too. They'd stood by him just as much as the man had, and been friendly too.

At least he could show them he didn't

have anything else to give, so he tipped his gourd out over his cupped palm. Several grains of salt glittered amid the other crumbs. Not nearly enough for a gift, but the women pressed eagerly forward and picked them out and put them on their tongues with little gasps of pleasure.

Po had a sudden thought. There was plenty of salt at the camp, if he could persuade them to come there. And then perhaps Po could fetch Tun and Suth and the others to meet the man. And then, wonderfully, he might show them the way through the marshes.

And it would be all Po's doing.

Before the women could grab the last couple of grains, he closed his fingers over them and held them tight. With his other hand he tapped the knuckles, and then pointed out across the mud.

The women were trying to pry his fingers open, laughing at their game. He snatched his fist out of reach and pointed again and made the encouraging *food* noises that Porcupine parents used to call their children to come and eat.

They stopped laughing and stared at him, and at his cupped hand when he opened it and showed them the salt and pointed again. They stared out at the dimly seen slope of hill beyond the mudbank, and he realized they'd understood.

So had the man, and he obviously didn't like the idea. The women took his hands and wheedled, but he pulled them away, grunting angrily. They fell on their knees and stroked him and fawned on him, until he gave a heavy, exasperated sigh and led the way onto the last hidden path.

Oldtale

The Father of Snakes

Tov journeyed north. The parrot sat on his head. It slept. The sun shone on their right, and was over them, and they came to a great hole. Beside it was a tree, a tree of the desert, that does not die. This was the place of Fododo, the Father of Snakes.

Tov said, "Hide, little parrot. Birds are snake food."

The parrot flew into the tree and hid.

Tov put his hands to his mouth and called, loud, loud, "Fododo, come out of your hole."

Fododo heard, and came. His body was ten and ten paces long,

and ten and ten and ten more. His width
was the width of a man's body, and his color
was white, like bone, an old bone in the
desert.

He looked at Tov, and the look was
magic. Tov could not move.

Fododo said, "Tov, you are a great fool."

Tov said, "You know my name. How is
this?"

Fododo said, "I know all, all."

Tov said, "I, Tov, know a thing. You,
Fododo, do not know it. It is this. There is
one. Day comes. This one has laughter and
no words. She has wings and no arms. Night
comes. This one has words; she has laughter.
She has arms and no wings. Fododo, Father
of Snakes, who is this one? You do not
know."

It was true, and thus Fododo lost his
magic. Above his head the parrot cried. Its
cry was laughter. Fododo looked up, and
Tov could move. He ran behind the tree,
quick, quick.

The parrot flew down in front of the head
of Fododo. He struck at her, but she flew
behind him. He followed her with his head,
close, close, but she flew under and over and

around, and again, and yet again. All the time Fododo followed her with his head.

Then she flew up into the tree, and he reached to catch her. But his body was now a great knot. Reaching, he pulled it tight, so that he could not move.

Tov came out from behind the tree, and went behind Fododo and took him by the neck. Fododo opened his mouth to bite him, but Tov was ready. He thrust his digging stick between the jaws of Fododo, from the side, so that the poison fangs were in front of the stick.

Tov took hold of the left fang and pulled hard, hard. The fang came out, and Tov held it and rejoiced. He took his stick from the jaws of Fododo. Still Fododo could not move.

Tov said, "Come, little parrot, we have finished." He left.

Fododo called after him, "Tov, be careful, careful. My fang is full of death."

Tov answered, "Fododo, you are right. But it is not the death of Tov, nor of his parrot."

8

By now it was midmorning. Po guessed that everyone would be foraging down at the inlet, but as he led the way up the slope he heard a shout to his left and saw Mana running toward him. He made *Wait* signs to the marshpeople and raced to meet her. They flung their arms around each other and hugged close. Po was so happy to see her that it took him a while to realize she was sobbing.

He held her by the shoulders and looked at her.

"You cry, Mana," he said. "Why is this? I come back. I am happy, happy."

"Oh, Po," she sobbed. "I look for you long, long. I say in my heart, *Po is dead*. I am sad, sad."

She took his hand.

"Come," she said. "See Suth, see Noli, see Tinu. Oh, Po, we are sad!"

"No," he said. "First you greet these people. They bring me back. Mana, they are like Tor. They do not have words. Then I take them to our lair. I give them salt. It is my thank gift. You go to Suth. You tell him, *Po is back*."

He took her to meet the marshpeople, and she kneeled and pattered her hands on the ground in front of the man, as she would have on greeting an important man from the Kin. He looked puzzled but more confident. There was no way he could be afraid of Mana.

She rose and put her arms around Po and made *Thank-you* sounds to the women, and then ran off, while Po led the way on. The moment they reached the ridge and could see the camp below them, the man halted and gave a sharp bark. All three stared wide-eyed down the slope. Po followed their gaze, bewildered. There was nobody down at the camp, nothing but the embers of the fire and the crocodile head on its pole....

Of course, the crocodile head! Po remembered what a celebration there'd been when the marshpeople had brought home the little crocodile they'd caught—and the crocodile heads on the poles around the entrance to their lair, none of them anything like the size of this monster.

The man turned and stared at Po. Po smiled confidently.

"We kill the crocodile," he said. "Our women do it. I, Po, help."

He tapped himself on the chest. It was good to be able to boast a bit in front of this man, after all that groveling and pleading in the marshes. He made the *Come* sound and started down the slope. The marshpeople followed, murmuring doubtfully and then hanging back and finally stopping completely.

Po waited. He wasn't impatient. He needed them still to be here when Suth came, because that would put off the time when Po had to face him alone. And surely, however bad he'd been, Suth would see that some good had come of it, and be easier on him because, after all, he had found the marshpeople. Didn't that count for something?

So he watched the man gesture to the women to stay where they were, and then walk with slow, stiff strides toward the crocodile head. A few paces from it he stopped and barked, three times, with long pauses between each bark. Then he kneeled and crawled to the pole and knocked his forehead on the ground at its foot, and finally rose and stood directly in front of the monster. He raised his right arm in a kind of salute and stood in silence for a while.

Very slowly, like a man going through some kind of big test in front of his whole Kin, he moved his hand forward and rested the fingers against the monster's snout, waited a little, and withdrew it. Still saluting, he took several slow paces backward, kneeled and knocked his forehead on the ground again, and then rose and came back to the women.

They fawned on him as usual, but this time with gentle, wondering movements, as if he were part of something magical. Each of them took a hand, and together they led him to join Po and then went on into the camp, where they carefully sat him down as if he couldn't do even that for himself.

Po didn't interrupt. He had some idea what was happening. Noli often needed help like that after Moonhawk had come to her. The man had been doing First One stuff. So Po quietly went and fetched three small blocks of salt from under the rock where it was stored, and then waited until the man gave a violent shudder, and sneezed, and shook his head and stared around as if he had no idea where he was, until his eye fell on the crocodile and he remembered.

He grunted and looked questioningly at Po. Po went over and formally presented him with the largest chunk of salt. The man took it and thanked him and then just as formally gave Po back his own cutter, and Po thanked him as if he'd never seen it before. Quickly he gave the two women their salt. They crowed with delight, but instead of thanking him they fawned on him, the same way they did on the man, while the man looked on benignly.

They hadn't finished when Po saw Suth loping up from the inlet. He signed to the man to stay where he was and ran to meet him. Suth stopped and waited, making Po come to him. Po had seen him looking angry before, but never so stern.

"Oh, Suth," he gasped, "I am bad, bad. I, Po, know this. But hear me. I went to the marsh. I found people. Suth, they live in the marsh. They know all its paths. Three brought me back, one man, two women. Suth, they are here. Come greet them. Perhaps they show us the way through the marsh."

Po's voice trailed away. Suth didn't answer. Beyond him Po could see Noli, Tor, Bodu and her baby, Tinu, Mana, and Tan coming up the hill. Tor was carrying Tan on his shoulders.

"Po, you are bad, bad," said Suth. "I tell you later. Come."

On the way back to the camp Po explained as much about the marshpeople as there was time for—how they didn't have words but used sounds and gestures like Tor and the Porcupines, and the men colored their faces like demons, and they mostly ate raw fish because they didn't have fire, and the crocodile was some kind of First One, and so on. Suth said nothing.

They found the three marshpeople standing close together with the man in front. He looked very tense, and was holding his fishing stick point down but ready to raise and strike. Moving calmly and confidently Suth laid his digging stick on the ground and walked forward with his right hand raised, palm forward, fingers spread.

As he reached the man he made a low humming noise in his throat. This was how the Porcupines greeted each other when two men met.

Instead of the hum, the man gave a soft bark, but his gesture was the same as Suth's, and the two men touched palms. Po sighed with relief. So far, so good.

Next Suth put his arm around Po's shoulders and drew him against his side and made *Thank-you* noises, and then presented the man with his cutter. The man gave him in exchange two of the wooden tubes from his belt. Suth looked at them, puzzled, and the man took them back and struck them against each other, showing that they made a sweet, ringing noise. Smiling, he beat out a pattern of sound with them, *tic-atic-tack*, *tic-atic-tack*, and Po recognized the strange woodpecker sound that had reached him across the water when the hunters were carrying the crocodile home. Suth smiled and took the tubes and tried for himself, while the man made encouraging murmurs.

By now Noli and the others had arrived. While Tor greeted the man, the rest of them hugged Po, laughing and crying, and then bowed and fluttered their fingers to the man and went to greet the women. In no time, Noli and the older woman were stroking each other's rounded bellies with admiring coos and a lot of laughter from the other three.

Then they all sat down, and Mana passed around a small gourd of seed paste, and showed the marshpeople how to dip a finger into it and lick the paste off. But before long the marshman started to become restless, and as soon as Suth stood up he jumped up too and called to his women to come.

Before he left the camp he kneeled in front of the crocodile head again, and rose and touched his fingertips to the crocodile's snout, and to his own forehead, and then backed away.

Suth and Po walked down to the marsh with the visitors, and on the way Suth tried to get the man to understand that he needed someone to act as a guide across to the far side, but the man didn't understand, so they made *Good-bye* noises on the bank, and watched the marshpeople pick their way along the hidden path until they disappeared into the haze.

"Now, Po, I speak to you," said Suth, and told him in a quiet, even voice, without anger or contempt, how bad he had been. It was very bad indeed. Po wept.

They walked up the slope in silence, but before they reached the camp, Suth said, "Hear me, Po. Soon people come to rest. Tun calls you. He says, *Po, tell what you have done. Tell what you have seen.* You tell all. Think now of your words. But hear me, Po. You were lucky, lucky. Lucky does not boast."

"Suth, I hear," said Po. It struck him that Suth could have waited until everyone was there and then told Po in front of them all how bad he'd been. He was very grateful that he hadn't, but that didn't make it any easier when Po had to stand in front of Tun and the others and tell his story. Even Kern looked horrified as Po explained how he'd glimpsed the marshman and crawled out across the dangerous mud and tried to reach him, without telling anybody.

But as soon as he got to the meeting, their faces changed, and they started to ask questions. And when he told how the women had tried to lick and rub the darkness off his skin, somebody laughed, and he started to feel better.

There were a lot more questions. The rest time lasted halfway through the afternoon, and then Po took everyone down to the marsh and showed them the hidden pathway. It was easy to find now, because the dried mud near the shore was still trampled where Po and the marshpeople had crossed it, but farther out the wet mud had closed over their footprints, and there was no trace at all.

They foraged until dark. Po felt wonderfully happy to be back where he belonged, among friends. To his surprise Nar came to talk to him and asked several questions, and then laughed and said, "Po, I think you find the way through the marsh. Soon I give you my gift."

"Tomorrow is tomorrow," said Po loftily, and Nar laughed again.

Nothing much happened for the next two days. By now they'd almost stripped the inlet of food and would have liked to move on, but there was nowhere to go. Var and Net explored the way into the marsh, taking salt in case they met any of the marshpeople, but they got only as far as the first island, and Po's friends hadn't been there. They couldn't find the path to the next island.

On the third morning Po and Mana were deep in a thicket, excitedly digging out a burrow Mana had found. They were almost at the nest, and could hear the frenzied squeaking of the little creatures trapped below, when Suth called. Disappointed, Po wormed his way out and found Suth, with Tan standing puzzled beside him.

"Noli's baby begins its birth-time," explained Suth. "Men and boys go."

Po understood at once. The same thing had happened when Ogad had been born, a few moons back. It had been nighttime, and they'd been asleep, but Suth and Po and Tan and all the other males old enough to walk had left the lair and gone away into the dark and waited until they heard the birth song rising from around the fire. Then they'd gone back, and Suth had seen his baby son for the first time.

Childbirth, more than anything else, was woman stuff. Men and boys weren't allowed near it. Only small babies like Ogad could stay, because they were still feeding from the breast and needed their mothers. So now all the males trooped back up to the camp to wait in the mottled shade beneath the leafless trees. The men settled down to playing their usual game, tossing pebbles into a circle drawn in the dirt and trying to knock someone else's pebble out of the circle.

Po was very restless. After his adventure in the marsh he'd promised he wouldn't go out of Suth's sight without permission. There was nothing he wanted to do under the trees. He was too young to join in the game. He had no one to play with, only Nar. He had begun to feel different about Nar since their strange little conversation a few days back, but he didn't know how to start making friends after working so hard at being enemies for so long.

Po went and watched the game until Suth had finished his turn, and then kneeled beside him and whispered, "Suth, I go up the hill. I look at the marsh. I stay there. I do not go down to the marsh. I, Po, ask."

Suth glanced at him. Po could see he was trying not to smile. "Go, Po," he said, and turned back to the game.

So Po climbed to his watch place and sat with his back to a boulder, staring longingly out over the marshes. He could just see the tops of the trees on the island where he'd met the marshman. So close... Perhaps the man was there again, at this very moment.... Suppose Po borrowed the sound sticks he'd given to Suth and went down to the shore and banged them together....

He'd hardly got into the dream when Nar came and squatted beside him.

"What do you do, Po?" he asked.

"I wait," said Po. "Perhaps I see something. Perhaps I hear something."

"I wait with you?" asked Nar.

"Good," said Po and made room for him to put his back against the boulder. Below them the marshes steamed in silence.

After a while Nar said, "My mother, Zara, is sad, sad. All of our Kin are gone. Dead. Lost. We lived on the mountain. We were happy. The mountain burned. It threw up great rocks. One hit my father, Beg. He died. We fled. We came to a desert, no food, no water. Many died there. My sister, Illa, died. Others were lost. Now my mother says to me, *We two are all our Kin. Here is little food. Soon it is gone. Then we die. You die, my son, Nar. Then our Kin is dead.* Po, my mother is sad, sad."

Po murmured sympathetically. He remembered the strange feeling he'd had when Cal had been killed by the crocodile. His whole Kin, Fat Pig, had died with him. Until that moment there'd always been a Fat Pig Kin, ever since the First Ones had raised the children of An and Ammu in the First Good Place. Po could imagine how he would feel if he knew that he was the last of Moonhawk and there would be no more after him. It would be worse than his own death.

No wonder Nar was so interested in finding a way through the marshes.

Po couldn't think of anything to say, so they sat in silence. Though there was no wind, the haze over the marshes seemed to move around all the time, with thicker and thinner patches coming and going. At times Po could see the dim outlines of several islands, but a few moments later they would all have vanished.

He was getting restless again when Nar straightened, peered, and pointed.

"A thing comes," he whispered. "People? Animals?"

Po stared, and he too saw the vague, dark shape coming slowly through the haze toward the land. It was roughly where the hidden path was. It was too big to be an animal. It could only be several people, moving close together.

Both boys rose. Po took a couple of paces down the hill. In the nick of time he remembered his promise to Suth. He turned, and together they raced back to the men, and kneeled and rapped their knuckles together. The men looked up, frowning at the interruption.

"Tun, I, Nar, speak," said Nar, and at once went on without waiting for permission. "People come from the marsh. Po sees this also."

The men snorted with surprise, broke off their game, and ran up to the ridge. By the time they got there, the vague shape that Nar and Po had seen had reached the shore and was clearly visible. It was indeed people. Seven or eight marshmen. They formed a line and marched up the hill with their fishing sticks gripped menacingly above their shoulders.

Oldtale
Tov and Falu

Tov came to Stonejaw. The parrot was with him. The rock still held the mouth of Stonejaw so that it could not close. Tov went into the mouth and found water. He drank and filled his gourd and left the cave. Beside Stonejaw he camped and ate meat from the gazelle. Night came.

Tov said, "Now I sleep, little parrot. Keep watch."

He lay down and slept.

It was dark, and the parrot was Falu again. Now she sang with her own voice. These were the words of her song:

> Parrot, First One,
> I am your nestling.
> You brood over me.
> You bring me sweet fruits.
> It is day, I am a parrot.
> It is night, I am a child.
> Let me be these no more.
> Make me a woman.

Then Falu went into the cave, into the mouth of Stonejaw. She washed the yellow feathers from her buttocks, and the gray dust from her body, and made herself clean. When she left the cave she was a woman.

Tov slept. All night Falu watched over him.

In the morning Tov woke and saw Falu. He did not know her.

He said, "Now, woman, I see you. Tell me your name."

She said, "I am Falu, daughter of Dat. I was a child. She is gone. I was a parrot, a little gray parrot with yellow tail feathers. It is gone. I am here. Tov, I choose you for my mate. Do you choose me?"

Tov said in his heart, *Gata is more beautiful, but Falu is clever, clever. She is brave. She helps me.* He said, "Falu, I choose you for my mate. Now we smear salt on our brows."

Falu said, "No, Tov, we wait. My father, Dat, has my promise. He chooses for me. Now we go to him. You give him your gift, the tooth of Fododo, Father of Snakes, the poison tooth. You say to him, *Give me Falu for my mate.*"

Tov said, "I do this. It is good."

Tov and Falu journeyed together. The sun was in their faces. They were happy, happy.

9

The marshmen came steadily up the hill. Their whole bodies, not just their faces and hands, were blobbed and streaked with demon colors.

The Kin men massed to face them. A low growl rose from their throats, and their hair began to bush out.

The marshmen's hair bushed in answer. They didn't growl but made a weird, high yapping sound that was just as frightening.

Halfway between the two parties, Po watched, appalled. The marshmen were going to pass only a few paces from him, but they weren't looking at him. He mightn't have been there at all.

Without warning, Net yelled and charged down the hill. Tun shouted at him to stop, but Net charged on. The marshmen halted. Their throwing arms went back.

Po had seen what those fishing sticks could do, how sharp they were, how far the marshmen could throw them. Without thought he dashed forward, shouting a warning.

"Danger! Sticks are sharp, Net, sharp!"

He stood in Net's path, shouting and waving his arms. Crazy. How could a child stop a grown man in a fighting rage, the rage of a hero? Net charged straight through him.

Po was slammed aside and flung sprawling down the slope. The breath whooshed out of him. He lay stunned, bruised, croaking for air. His head seemed full of a strange whooping sound.

As he struggled to his feet he realized that the sound was coming from outside him. Dazedly he looked around. Net was lying facedown on the slope just below him. Dead? No. He was trying to get up, but croaking and gasping, even worse winded than Po had been. Just beyond him stood the marshmen. They had lowered their sticks, and their hair was no longer bushed. With their free hands they were pointing at Net and whooping with laughter. Tears streamed down their bright-colored faces. Some were stamping their feet, and others were almost doubled up. They were helpless. If the Kin men had attacked now, they couldn't have fought back.

Bewildered, Po turned. The Kin men had lowered their digging sticks and their hair too was starting to lie down. Kern was smiling and shaking his head. Po saw Tun speak to Var and beckon to Tor, and then walk calmly down the slope with Tor beside him. Bruised and scraped and still totally bewildered, Po helped Net to his feet and fetched his digging stick for him. Net didn't seem to want to fight anyone now. They waited to see what Tun would do.

A few paces from the marshmen he halted and signed to Tor to do the same. They laid their digging sticks on the ground and walked on, with their right hands raised, palms forward, the sign of peace. They halted again and waited for the laughter to end. Po thought Tor looked anxious, but Tun seemed quite confident. As soon as he could make himself heard without shouting, he turned and spoke to Net.

"Go back, Net. Take Po. I, Tun, speak."

Obediently Net limped up the hill, not

looking at Po. Po could feel his shame, that he had let himself be so jeered at by these strangers. He couldn't imagine anything more awful. He was afraid Net was now very angry with him, because Po had got in the way of his hero charge down the hill. What was Po, a stupid little boy, doing meddling with man stuff?

Kern came to meet them and put his arm around Net and consoled him as he limped back to his friends. Trailing anxiously behind, Po saw Suth beckon. By the time he reached him, Suth was busy watching Tun and Tor dealing with the marshmen.

"Suth, what happens?" he whispered. "Do we fight the marshmen?"

"No. You, Po, stopped the fighting."

"I think Net is angry with me for this. Am I bad, Suth?"

Suth snorted, amused.

"No, Po. This time you are not bad."

Po was relieved, but still baffled. Only a few minutes ago everything had seemed so terrifying and hopeless, but now...

"Why do the marshmen laugh, Suth?" he asked. "Why do you smile?"

"Po, I cannot say. This was laughter stuff, that is all. Net charges. It is a hero charge.

Who can stop him? A boy stands in his path. The boy waves his arms; he shouts. The hero does not see the boy. He hits him, he falls, he cannot breathe. The hero is gone…. I see it, I laugh. It is laughter stuff…. Ah, see, we do not fight. They come. Now Tun gives them salt."

Po looked and saw Tun leading the way up the hill, waving to the marshmen to follow. They did so, keeping close together, silent and purposeful, and not seeming at all friendly, but not in the fighting postures in which they had first arrived. Now Po recognized their leader as his friend from the marshes, but the man didn't seem to notice him.

As they crossed the ridge, the leader gave a loud bark and stopped dead. The others lined up on either side of him. Tun turned and waited. The marshmen paid no attention to him. A low, astonished moan came from their lips. Po realized what was happening. They had seen the great crocodile head for the first time.

"Suth," he whispered. "They do not come for salt. They come for our crocodile."

"Po, you are right," muttered Suth. "I tell Tun."

He caught Tun's eye, and the two men moved aside and talked quietly together. Tun nodded and went on down toward the camp.

With slow, stiff steps the marshmen approached the great head and halted a few paces in front of it. One by one they kneeled, crawled forward, knocked their foreheads on the ground at the foot of the pole, then rose and touched their fingertips to the vicious snout and their own foreheads. They stood for a while, breathing deeply, and walked backward to their places in the line. Just as Po had done, the Kin men recognized all this as First One stuff, and watched in silence.

The leader came last. He also took a few paces backward, but instead of returning to the line he halted and came forward again, with his hands raised in front of him, obviously now intending to lift the head from the pole. Po heard murmurs of anger from the Kin men. This wasn't right. It wasn't the marshmen who'd killed the crocodile, it was Chogi and the women. The head belonged to the Kin. Po started to feel anxious again. Was there going to be fighting after all?

But Tun had other ideas. As the marshman had been moving back, he had come and waited beside the pole. Now, before the marshman reached it, he lifted the head free and carried it forward to meet him. Startled, the marshman halted.

Tun held out the head and made the double hum in his throat that meant *I give*. The man stared, even more astonished, and then reverently took the head and made his *I am pleased* sound, loudly, three times.

The whole line of marshmen made noises of wonder and delight as the leader carried the head back to them. He laid it carefully on the ground, hesitated, picked up his fishing stick, and looked at Tun. Suddenly he seemed unsure of himself. Po could see just what he was thinking. He didn't have a gift nearly magnificent enough to offer in exchange for the crocodile head. Would Tun accept the fishing stick, or would he be offended?

But Tun was ready for this. He made a *Come* noise, beckoned to Tor, and led the way back up to the ridge.

"Nar, Po," said Suth. "Go. Find the women. Say to Chogi, *Wait for Noli's baby. Then come quick, quick. Bring food.*"

"What happens?" asked Po as he and Nar loped down toward the inlet.

"Tun spoke with Suth," said Nar. "I heard their words. Tun gives the head of the crocodile. This is his gift. The marshman gives the path through the marshes. That is his gift. Now Tor says this to him."

Po understood at once. Though he and all the Kin knew the Porcupines well and were expert at using their sounds, it was still often impossible to get them to understand something that the Kin could explain to each other in a few words. But the Porcupines had ways of doing it among themselves, with a lot of touching and grunting and gestures, until they agreed on whatever it was. Po's friend must have done something like this to persuade the other marshmen to join him on his expedition to fetch the crocodile head. And Tor would have the best chance, now, of explaining to him what Tun wanted.

As they neared the inlet, Po heard the sound of women's voices, singing high and happy, rising and falling in waves, three or four voices together, others lacing in and taking over, then a single voice, the chief woman's, Chogi's, ringing with joy, and the first voices answering again, and yet again—the Newborn Girl Song that the daughters of An and Ammu in the Oldtales had invented to sing together when Turka's first child was born.

They halted and waited. It was too soon for men or boys to be let anywhere near the birthplace, however urgent the message. As the last notes died, Mana came running toward them.

"Noli's baby is born!" she cried. "It is a girl. She is beautiful, beautiful. Nar, Po, why are you here? What happens?"

"A big thing happens, Mana," said Nar. "Go. Find Chogi. Tell her *Come quick*."

Mana hesitated a moment, but she could see this wasn't just boy stuff. Nar was serious. She scampered back down among the thickets. A little later Chogi appeared, frowning even more deeply than usual, obviously displeased by the interruption of important woman stuff. Impatiently at first, she listened to Nar's explanations, but then nodded and said, "This is good. The birth is easy. Noli is strong. We come soon. Tell this to Tun. Now, go."

When the boys got back to the camp they

found that Tun and Tor had somehow persuaded the marshmen to guide them into the marsh. Now, while they waited for the women, the men were sitting in the shade of the trees, with the crocodile head perched on a nearby boulder, teaching the marshmen how to play the pebble game.

Before long the women arrived. Noli, tired but laughing with happiness, showed Tor his daughter. Tor hugged and stroked her, and then carried the baby around to show to the men, coming to Po last of all. As far as Po was concerned, the baby was just a baby, wrinkled and floppy the way newborn babies always were. Her skin was paler than Noli's dark brown, much nearer the tan color of Tor and the Porcupines. Po made the correct *Praise* sounds while Tor beamed with pride and delight.

Meanwhile the Kin shared food with their visitors. Nobody got more than a mouthful or two, as the store was almost empty and they hadn't foraged long that morning before Noli's baby had started to come. But it was important to do everything they could to signal to the marshmen that they wanted them to be friends and allies. To make up for the scanty meal, Tun gave each of the visitors a palmful of salt, and they were delighted.

Now it was time to go. While the Kin packed their gourds with anything they had to carry, and Po helped Tinu fill and seal the fire log, the visitors laid two of their fishing sticks side by side on the ground, settled the crocodile head between them, and lashed it firm with reed leaves. When they were ready, their leader arranged them in single file, pushing them around till he had them where he wanted.

Po watched, fascinated. Only five days ago this man had let himself be driven back to his island by the other marshmen, but now he was completely in command, and nobody questioned him. It was because of the crocodile head, Po guessed. He had discovered it, and now Tun had given it to him. That made him a big man, important.

When he was satisfied, the leader barked, once. The two men at the head of the line bent and picked up the fishing sticks and lifted them onto their shoulders, one at each end, with the crocodile head sagging between them. The leader took two of the wooden tubes from his belt, and the four men at the back did the same. He placed himself at the head of the procession and marched off, rattling his tubes together as he went. The four at the back joined in and the whole line followed him up to the ridge, with the Kin, men, women, and children, trailing behind.

As the haze-hidden marsh came in sight, the leader gave a shout of triumph, and the other six answered with cries of praise. A few paces farther they repeated it, and again and again as they marched down the slope.

Po found the noises strangely exciting. The woodpecker sound of the tubes had a kind of pattern in it, and the cries were part of the pattern. There was a meaning there too, almost as clear as he had learned to hear in the grunts and barks of the Porcupines. The meaning was happiness. It was glory.

Oldtale

Tov's Gift

Tov and Falu journeyed all day and came to Bagworm. His water lay beside him. His mouth was full of dirt, and he could not suck it away. There were fish in the water. Tov and Falu took them and ate and drank and filled their gourd. Bagworm saw this. He was very angry.

Night came. Tov and Falu kept watch in turn, each while the other slept. They woke, they journeyed, they came to Twoheads. His heads fought still, and the yellow blood dripped from them. Tov and Falu drank it and filled their gourd. Night came, and they slept and kept watch as before.

They woke, they journeyed, they came to Tarutu Rock. Weaver camped there, Tov's own Kin. Tov said, "Tell me, my kinspeople, where is Dat?"

They answered, "Parrot camps at Dead Trees Valley. He is there."

Tov and Falu journeyed to Dead Trees Valley. When Gata saw them coming she hid, close, in long grasses.

Tov stood before Dat and said, "Dat, I bring you the gift you ask. I bring you the tooth of Fododo, Father of Snakes. I bring you the poison tooth. Here is Falu, your daughter. She is a woman. I choose her for my mate. She chooses me. Dat, do you say *Yes* to this?"

Dat said, "Give me the tooth of Fododo, Father of Snakes. Give me the poison tooth."

Tov gave him the tooth. Dat held it in his hand. He said, "My promise was not for Falu. It was for Gata. I say *No* to your choosing."

Tov was very angry. He said, "Give me back my gift."

Dat said, "The gift is given. It is mine."

He closed his hand on the tooth, tight, tight, so that it bit into his palm and the poison went into his blood. He died.

Then Tov and Falu smeared salt on their brows, and were chosen.

All this Gata saw and heard, hiding in the long grasses.

10

Slowly the procession picked its way along the hidden pathway. By the time everyone was ashore on the first island the buried reeds were beginning to give way, from so many people crossing all together. The crossing to the second island was worse. They had to hold hands and form a human chain to pull the last of them safely through.

The marshmen paid no attention but strutted on ahead. They were well out of sight by now, though their wild music still floated eerily across the marsh. The Kins hurried after the sound and saw them disappearing across a mudbank into the haze ahead. But the marshman's two mates were there, waiting to help. They were obviously amazed to see so many people winding out from the trees, but the younger of them recognized Po and ran to greet him, marsh fashion, with hugging and stroking.

She crowed with delight over Noli's baby and called to the other woman to come and admire her, and then they set about organizing the next crossing. They made the Kins go over a few at a time, with each party carrying a bundle of reeds to tread in anywhere the path felt weak. With plenty of workers, and cutters to gather the reeds, this didn't take long, but even so the sound of the marshmen's procession grew steadily fainter as they drew ahead.

Then it started to get louder again, and the Kins actually caught up on the far side of the fifth island, where several people had been fishing along a channel of open water, and the marshmen had stopped so that the men there could do First One stuff with the crocodile head. They were just finishing when the Kins came up with them.

The women ran to look at the strangers, and clucked and cooed over the baby, though some of them made sorrowful sounds and looked Noli in the eyes and sighed sympathetically.

"Why are they sad, Po?" asked Mana.

"Mana, I do not know," he answered. "I think they say, *It is only a girl. A boy is better.*

For them, men are big, big. Women are small. See, these new ones. Three men. Five, six women. I told you this. The women are the men's mates. A man has two mates, or three. It is strange, strange."

Mana was staring at him, wide-eyed. Perhaps she hadn't taken it in, hadn't really believed it, when he'd explained about it earlier.

"Po, this is not good," she whispered.

He heard mutters of agreement from around and realized that several of the others had been listening, Yova and Var as well as his own family. Suth nodded encouragingly to him. It was a curious feeling for Po, being listened to as if what he had to say was something his hearers wanted to know about. He was pleased but at the same time uncomfortable. It was as if he had been somehow changed by his adventure, but wasn't quite ready for the change.

All afternoon the procession threaded its way across the marsh, going more and more slowly as it picked up fresh followers. The men joined at the front and added to the patterned din, while the women and children thronged laughing behind. By the time they reached the central camp, the line was snaking almost across two islands and the channel between them.

Already the sun was a fuzzy blob low down on their left, all the shrouding haze glowed gold, and the lake surrounding the island shimmered with the colored light. Across its shining surface Po watched the men at the head of the procession move onto the raised path to the islands. Their reflections moved with them, scarcely rippling on the silky water. The echoes of their music floated away over the distant reedbeds. Five of them now were carrying the crocodile head at arm's length above their heads. Even seen at that distance through the marsh haze it looked a fierce and dreadful thing. Po shuddered, remembering his nightmares. He well understood why this was First One stuff for the marshmen.

A small procession came out to meet the main one and did their greeting in the middle of the pathway, then turned and led the trophy home, with the whole long line of people shuffling behind. The music, tens and tens and tens of marshmen rattling their soundsticks and shouting their cries, didn't stop for an instant. By the time the Kins reached the pathway it was dusk.

They found the area around the entrance to the main island already crowded with excited people, so they pushed their way through to the farther side and settled down where they could hear themselves talk.

"We were eight Kins at Odutu," Po heard Chogi say. "All of the Kins, men and women and children. Yet these marshpeople are more."

"Chogi, you are right," said Kern. "But what do we eat? We have little food here."

"We eat fish," said Suth. "Come, Kern. Come, Zara. Come, Mana and Po. Bring salt. Po, you know these people. You say to the women, *You give me fish. I give you salt.*"

It was still just light enough to see. The women were sitting in groups, with the fish they'd caught piled between them. Suth chose a group that seemed to have plenty, handed Po a chunk of salt, and gave him an encouraging pat on the shoulder.

Hesitantly, Po went over. The women were already watching him, nudging each other and making their chuckling noise of interest and amusement. He crumbled some grains of salt into his palm and offered them around. The women took them and put them to their tongues and begged for more. Po picked up a fish and made the *I ask* grunt. All the women grabbed for fish and thrust them at him, with eager *I give* noises. One by one he took them and passed them back to Suth and handed over another morsel of salt.

The job wasn't made any easier by the women who'd already had their share pinching and rubbing at his skin or scratching it with a fingernail to see if the color was real. He could hear Suth and the others laughing behind him as he tried to slap the hands away, not let go of the precious salt, and pass the slippery fish back to them.

They worked on from group to group. Sometimes one of the marshmen would come strutting up and bark at the women, who would give him a fish and fawn on him while he munched it. He paid no attention to Po and the others, and as soon as he'd eaten he'd strut away to rejoin the noise-makers.

By now it was fully dark, but when Po and his party got back to the others they found a fire going, with everyone scavenging along the shoreline for broken and discarded reed, which burned brightly but without much heat. Luckily there was masses of it, and after a while they were able to bury fish among the ashes and wait till they were cooked and rake them out with sticks to cool. They were delicious, as good as the crocodile tail had been that first night.

The marshpeople didn't seem to have fire, but they must have known about it, because soon they were coming with dry reeds and thrusting them into the blaze and then they ran with them to piles they'd already built and got their own fires going. By the time the Kins had finished eating, the island was dotted with patches of light, with dark figures moving to and fro between them. The brightest blaze of all was over by the entrance, where the main crowd was and where most of the noise came from.

Po was intrigued.

"Suth, we go see?" he begged.

Suth rose, saying, "Come, Tinu. Come, Mana and Tan. This is a thing to see. We do not see it again. Noli, do you come?"

In the end everyone came and joined the crowd at the entrance. None of the marshpeople paid any attention to them. Po couldn't see over all the bodies, but he managed to squirm his way through to the front. There he found an open space around the wall of crocodile skulls and the line of larger skulls on poles. The head of the monster crocodile was now on the central pole. In front of it a fierce fire blazed, with the firelight glinting off the ragged fangs and throwing flickering shadows across the scaly hide. The mass of marshmen stood in front of the wall, slamming their soundsticks together and yelling their cries. The women and children formed a circle around the scene. Inside this circle, one man strutted to and fro, leading the shouting and brandishing his fishing stick above his head every time he yelled.

Po didn't recognize him until a pregnant woman came up from the pathway and flung fresh reeds onto the fire and then fawned on him briefly. She was the older of the two women he'd met when he'd first found his way into the marsh. But then, a little later, a strange young woman appeared with more reeds and did the same. Before she'd finished, the younger of those first two women came with more reeds, and joined her. She didn't seem to mind about the other young woman being there already.

Po was watching this, open-mouthed, when the women he knew spotted him and dashed across and dragged him, laughing, in front of the man. Now Po could see by the firelight that it was indeed his friend, the man he'd met five days ago. He'd thought it must be, but he wouldn't have known him, with the mad, proud look on his face. His eyes were open so wide that the whites showed all the way around the irises, and the glisten of the flames added to the wildness.

Since noon the man had been leading the procession and then strutting in front of the crocodile head, all the time yelling his triumph cry. His voice was hoarse, his colored body shone with sweat and shuddered with effort, but he was still full of hero strength. He barely paused in his strut when he saw Po, but laughed and snatched him effortlessly into the air and sat him on his shoulder while he paraded around the ring.

Now Po found himself sucked into the frenzy, as he swayed above the heads of the crowd and looked out from the firelit island across the misty waters to the shadowy, dark distances of the marsh. He clutched the man's hair with his left hand and raised his right fist above his head and shook it to the beat of the soundsticks, and when the man yelled his cry he joined in at the top of his voice.

It was thrilling, a wonderful, wordless boast, a boast like no other boast that ever had been or ever would be, a boast to remember all his days, and there was no shame in it at all.

His throat was sore by the time the man at last put him down, and the crowd let him through and patted his back as he ran laughing to join his friends. They too were laughing, with him, not at him. They watched a little longer and then went back to their fire.

As they were lying down to sleep Po heard Var say, "This man makes a promise. He leads us through the marsh. Does he remember his promise tomorrow?"

"Var, I do not know," said Tun. "He is like a drinker of much stoneweed. Perhaps he remembers nothing."

They are wrong, Po thought. In the middle of his triumph the man had recognized Po. He'd known what he owed to him, even if Po hadn't done any of it on purpose. He would remember his promise.

Po was right. The man did remember. He came the next morning with his three mates and two other men and three more women—the two men's mates, Po guessed, though he didn't yet have a chance to work out who was whose. All of them carried fishing sticks, and the women had several fish strung on each of theirs.

Po's friend looked utterly exhausted, and when he tried to grunt or bark he made faint croaking sounds, but he still seemed completely sure of himself and greeted Tun as leader to leader. He let his senior mate make the *Come* sound, but he led the way off the island.

By now most of last night's crowd was gone, but the great crocodile head still stared grimly to the north, with the lesser heads on either side. The marshmen touched its snout reverently as they left. Po looked at it for the last time. It was just a crocodile head. Dead. It didn't scare him any more.

They had crossed only a few more islands when Po's friend halted and started to croak *Good-bye* sounds. After a moment's puzzlement Po realized from the way they were all behaving that his friends were now going to turn back, while the other five led the way on. The man presented Tun with the fishing stick one of his mates was carrying, with several fish on it, and Tun gave him a gourd and salt in exchange, with more salt for the women, and then with a great chorus of different sorts of Good-byes they parted.

Now the going was different, no longer islands and reedbeds with hidden pathways between them, but one endless vast reedbed where they trod not on squelching earth but on a solid network of reed roots just below the water. A maze of paths ran through it. Sometimes one of their guides would turn off down one of these, and a little later come hurrying up from behind with another fish to add to the collection.

Po was curious. He found the ways of the marshpeople weird but fascinating. So the next time one of the women turned off, he followed her. She heard him and looked back, but smiled and led the way on. Soon the side path ended. The woman put a finger to her lips, moved stealthily on, and kneeled beside a hole among the reed roots. From one of her belt tubes she sprinkled a few crumbs of something into the water, and then waited, motionless, with her fishing stick raised. Po saw her tense. She struck, and with an expert movement of her wrist twisted the spear so that the fish didn't flap itself off as she was pulling it out.

Po clapped his hands. She laughed and gave him the fish to carry as they ran to catch up with the others.

They took no midday rest but splashed steadily on, passing fish down the line to eat. Po had never known this kind of moist heat. The haze was so dense that it was hard to breathe. Insects swarmed. Sweat streamed down. There was a kind of buzzing tingle in the air. It felt as if the haze was somehow being stretched, tauter and tauter, and at any moment it was going to rip apart from horizon to horizon and let the clear sky through.

Noli's baby was whimpering and wouldn't be comforted.

"Her head hurts," said Noli. "Rain comes."

"Noli, you are right," said Suth.

And then, in what seemed like the middle of nowhere, the procession halted. Po was near the tail of it and couldn't see what was happening, but after some while Tun and Chogi came back down the line with their guides. Po watched, puzzled, while they made *Good-bye* noises and exchanged yet more gifts. The marshpeople were obviously very anxious, and kept adding *Danger* sounds onto their farewells, but in the end they turned and went back the way they had come.

"They go no further," Tun explained. "They are afraid. There is a path. It is not good. It is old."

"Tun, what is this danger?" Bodu asked.

"Bodu, I do not know," he answered. "We go on. We see. We are careful."

After that they struggled slowly on along what had once been a good path but was now almost blocked with new reeds. And then Po came around a bend and saw that ahead of him the line of people seemed to be rising into the air. A moment later he realized that they were climbing a solid slope. The haze thinned. Now Po too was out of the reeds and climbing. Ahead of him he could see a whole hillside, strewn with rocks and boulders. This was the northern edge of the marshes. They had come through.

The Kin stood and looked around. The

sun was already low. They were standing on what seemed to be a spur of hill jutting out into the marsh, so that both east and west they looked out over the same haze-hidden reeds. Though the hillside itself seemed barren, the shore was lined with thickets, but before he would let them forage Tun sent scouts up the hill and along the edges of the marsh. They returned saying that the promontory seemed to stretch a long way north but they had seen no sign of danger.

"The marshpeople were afraid," said Chogi. "Why is this?"

"They know this place," said Var in his gloomiest tones. "It is dangerous. We do not see this danger. It is here."

"Var speaks," said Kern, and they all laughed as usual, but nervously. The very stillness and emptiness of the hillside seemed a little menacing.

"I say this," Kern went on. "They are marshpeople. They do not like hard ground. It is not their Place."

There were murmurs of agreement, but all the same Tun sent Shuja and Nar to keep lookout while most of the others foraged along the shoreline for what they could find until it was almost dark.

But Suth and his family gathered fuel and climbed the hill and chose a site for their camp in a hollow between two ridges, so that no stranger could see their fire from a distance. Now Tinu anxiously opened the fire log. The reeds they had burned the night before had turned to ash, not embers, but she had saved the few bits of wood they had found for this purpose. When she tipped the fire log out and blew on the blackened pile, a few sparks glowed, and she was able to nurse a flame from them.

So they all gathered around in the near dark, and sang the song that the Kins had .always sung whenever they moved to a fresh camp and relit their fire. Then they cooked their food and shared it. When they had eaten, Tun rose and held up a hand for silence.

"Hear me, Tun," he said. "I praise the boy Po. Often Po is foolish. Often he is bad. So it is with boys. But we cross the marshes. Po found the way. This was his deed. Now let Po speak. Let him boast."

Po hesitated, astonished, then rose. This time he didn't feel nervous or tongue-tied. He had had his great boast last night, sitting on the marshman's shoulder, and that was enough. He remembered something that Suth had said to him not long ago.

"I, Po, speak," he said. "Hear me. Tun is right. I was foolish. I was bad. But I was lucky, lucky. Lucky does not boast."

He sat down, feeling that this time he'd gotten it right. The others seemed to think so too, and cheered quietly and laughed without any jeering. He even saw Chogi smile at him and nod. He felt very good.

Nar came and squatted beside him and said, "Po, you keep your promise. You find the way through the marsh. Now you tell me my gift to you."

Po smiled teasingly at him.

"I tell you tomorrow," he said.

Oldtale
Gata and Nal

Gata said in her heart, My
father, Dat, is dead. My sister, Falu,
is a woman. She chooses a mate.
Now I, Gata, have no one.

Men came to Gata, from Little
Bat and from Ant Mother. They
said, "Gata, you are beautiful,
beautiful. I choose you for my
mate. Do you choose me?"

To each of them Gata answered, "I do not choose you."

In her heart she said, I choose
only Nal.

Gata left her Kin and journeyed
alone to Ragala Flat. Snake camped there. She waited and watched
until Nal hunted alone. Then she

stood before him and said, "Nal, I choose you for my mate. Do you choose me?"

Nal answered, "Gata, you are Parrot. I am Snake. This is not good. It is bad, bad."

Gata said, "*Good* is a word. *Bad* is a word. I do not know them. I know only this. I choose you, Nal, for my mate. I choose no other man, ever."

Nal looked at her. She was beautiful, beautiful.

He said, "Gata, how do we live? Who is our Kin? Nobody. Where are our Good Places? We have none. Where do we hunt? Where do we forage?"

She said, "We go far and far. Perhaps we find Good Places. Perhaps we die. I choose you, Nal. I choose also this."

Nal said, "Let it be so. I choose you, Gata, for my mate."

Then they smeared salt on their brows, and were chosen. Their Kins said to them, "This is bad, bad. Go far and far."

Gata and Nal went to the Dry Places, the Demon Places. They found no food and no water. They lay down together and said, "Tomorrow we die."

They slept, and Gata dreamed.

Parrot came to Gata in her dream, and sang. This was his song:

> Gata, my daughter, my nestling,
> I do not brood over you.
> I bring you no sweet fruits.
> Tomorrow you die.
> But I say this to you, this:
> There are Kins, men and women,
> They have children, they grow
>   old, they die.
> And their children, and their
>   children's children.
> They sit around fires, they tell
>   Tales.
> They speak your name, *Gata*.
> They say, *Beautiful, like Gata*.
> They are sad, sad.

The First Ones too were sad for Gata and Nal. They changed them.

Two rocks stand in the Dry Places, a day's journey and another day's beyond Ragala Flat. No other rock there is like them.

One rock is smooth and black. When the sun shines, see, it is full of bright stars. It is beautiful. It is Gata.

The other is tall and strong. It is Nal.

11

Everyone was exhausted with the long day of struggling through the marsh, and there seemed to be no immediate threat of danger, so Tun didn't set sentries, and they lay down thankfully to sleep by their fire.

In the middle of the night, with a colossal crash of thunder, the rain came. The sleepers leaped awake and stood and raised their arms to the sky and let the warm, dense downpour sluice over their bodies. Hastily Tinu packed the fire log before the precious embers could be dowsed. Then they trooped up out of the hollow and watched the jigging legs of lightning prance to and fro over the marshes while the thunder bellowed on and on.

The storm ended as suddenly as it had begun, and the dark hillside tinkled with streaming water, and the smell of rain on dry earth filled the night with sweetness, and Po lay down to sleep again on the soaked ground and thought, *Ah, this is good, good.*

He managed to wake himself early the next morning, in the first gray light. He knew exactly what he was going to do. He crept across to where Tinu lay and touched her gently on her shoulder.

She woke instantly, and he put a finger to his lips for silence and beckoned to her and stole away up the short slope and over the brow, out of sight of the others. While he waited for her to join him he studied the hillside for any sign of danger, but it seemed as empty as ever. Then he looked around for somewhere a little hidden and private, so that there wouldn't be any interruptions. The rain had washed the air so clear that he could see all the way across the marshes, and across the New Good Places, to a faint blue line that he knew must be Dry Hills, the range of mountains on the farther side of the southern desert, many days' journey away.

There were some promising-looking places among the bushes beside the marsh to his left, so when Tinu joined him he took her by the wrist and said firmly, "Come."

She stared at him, but he tugged at her arm, and she went obediently down the hill with him.

He found a little open space between some bushes and the marsh, well screened from up the slope. He studied the ground for paw prints, and sniffed the air, which carried scents richly after the rain. There was nothing to suggest any dangerous beast might be lurking close by.

"Wait here, Tinu," he said. "I bring you a thing."

Before she could object he scurried back up the hill. By now the camp was stirring. He caught Nar's eye and waved to him to join him. At once Zara called to ask Nar where he was going.

"I go with Po," Nar answered cheerfully, making it sound like boy stuff. "We have a thing to do."

Po led him a couple of paces down the slope. He put his hand in his gourd and drew it out with the fingers closed to hide what he was holding.

"Now I tell you the gift you give me," he said.

With his free hand he pointed toward the marsh.

"Tinu waits there," he said. "Go to her. Take this."

He opened his hand and showed Nar the palmful of salt he had prepared, the whitest he could find, crumbled fine and mixed with a little spit and seedpaste so that it would stick.

"This, Nar, is the gift you give me," he said. "You choose Tinu for your mate."

Nar stared at the salt.

"Po, I cannot do this," he said.

"You made your promise," said Po firmly. "On Odutu you made it, Odutu below the Mountain."

Nar started to smile, as if this were boy stuff he was now too old for. Po kept his face serious. What he was asking was perfectly fair. A gift didn't need to be a thing. It could also be a deed, a favor. Nar's smile faded. He knew that he had promised on Odutu below the Mountain, and that was something he couldn't go back on.

He turned his head for a moment and looked back toward the camp. From where they were standing, they could just see the heads of the people moving around in the hollow, and Po guessed Nar was looking to see if his mother was watching. He remembered how furious Zara had seemed when Chogi had first suggested that Nar and Tinu should choose each other. What, her lovely son, the last of his Kin, mate with this girl whose face was all twisted and wrong, and who couldn't even talk right! No! He could wait till Mana was old enough, or Sibi.

Nar had always been a very good son and done whatever his mother wanted. Zara wasn't going to like this at all.

He looked at Po and nodded.

"I do it," he said slowly. "Give me the salt. Come."

They walked together down the slope, but Po stopped before they reached the bushes.

"I stay," he whispered. "You go alone."

Nar seemed to be deep in thought, barely noticing where he put his feet on the rough hillside, but he nodded. Obviously it would be better for Tinu to think he was asking her of his own accord. Po waited till he was out of sight, then crept down until he could see Nar and Tinu through a screen of branches. He was just in time to watch Nar hold out his hand and offer Tinu the salt.

She stared at it. Her jaw moved to and fro, the way it did when she was too excited, or too upset, to force her mouth to make words. She took half a pace back. Now a branch hid her face from Po. As he moved to where he could see her again, a twig cracked beneath his foot.

At once Tinu's head turned. Po froze, cursing himself. Stupid, stupid Po, always getting it wrong just when it mattered. Oh, why hadn't he looked, like a hunter, to see where he was putting his foot?

Tinu was staring directly at him, though he was sure she couldn't see him behind the bushes. Her face went stiff. She turned back to Nar and mouthed a question—*Who is there?* Po guessed. Nar answered. Now a longer question. Oh, let him lie, let him lie! Let him tell Tinu that he, Nar, had asked Po to take Tinu there to wait for him so that he could offer her the salt without everyone watching. But of course he wouldn't. This was a way out for him, a way he could give his gift to Po and still not make his mother furious. Stupid, stupid Po, when he'd gotten everything else so right and then at the last minute spoiled it all.

Nar was speaking. Tinu listened. Once or twice Po had seen people's faces after they'd died. Tinu's was like that. When Nar finished she bowed her head and at the same time pushed away the hand that was holding the salt.

Nar stared at it, then turned and walked back the way he had come. Tinu looked up to watch him go. Her face was so twisted that it didn't seem like a human face at all. Tears streamed down it. Po couldn't bear to watch, but at the same time couldn't look away.

A few paces from Po, but still on the far side of the bushes, Nar stopped. The hand with the salt moved gently up and down, as if he were judging its weight so that he could throw it as fiercely as possible into Po's face. He had the look of a grown man, the same look that Suth had had when he'd told Po how bad he'd been, going out into the marshes alone.

"Hear me, Po," he said, just loudly enough for Po to catch the words. "I, Nar, speak. My gift to you is given. I promised upon Odutu, Odutu below the Mountain. It is done. Now go. Go back to the others."

"I go," whispered Po miserably, and trudged back up the hill.

He couldn't bear to face anyone, so he climbed across the slope and around to the far side of the spur. He sat down well below the ridge, put his chin on his fists, and stared glumly west.

It was a wonderful day. He couldn't remember a day like this, so clear, so fresh. The marsh stretched limitlessly away, first the immense reedbed, and then the maze of islands and mudbanks and channels. Birds rose in flocks, circled, settled. The air was full of their calls. Another rainstorm was massing in the distance, a black bank of cloud trundling slowly toward him with its veil of rain beneath it. To the left and right of it rose the outer ends of a rainbow, and between them flashed the sudden spikes of lightning. Already he could hear the unsteady burr of thunder.

Wonderful, but Po barely saw it. All he could think of was that he had ruined his chances, and—far, far worse—ruined Tinu's chance of happiness. Everything was pointless, stupid, and it was all Po's fault.

Vaguely he noticed the voices of people, chattering excitedly. Something must be happening in the camp, but he wasn't interested. It didn't matter. Nothing mattered. If they'd never gotten across the marshes, if they'd all died in the desert, it wouldn't have been any worse.

A hand touched his shoulder. He looked around, ready to snap. It was Mana, with a broad smile on her face. Even Mana was laughing at him for being so stupid.

"Go!" he snarled.

She shook her head, still smiling.

"Come, Po," she said. "Suth says this. Come now."

She took his wrist, dragged him to his feet, and started to pull him up the slope. He came, grudging every step. From the ridge they looked down into the hollow.

Po couldn't make out what was happening. Everyone was massed in an excited group on the other side of the fire. He could see Tun and Chogi and Suth near the center, talking to a woman who had her back to him. Chogi was speaking earnestly to her.

The woman shook her head angrily. From the way she did it, Po recognized her as Zara. Chogi went on speaking till Tun held up his hand and spoke briefly to Zara.

He moved aside to make space for someone standing behind him. Nar.

Nar and Tinu were standing close

together with their fingers laced into each other's. Tinu, of course, had her head bowed to one side with shyness, but Nar faced his mother directly. He began to speak to her, firmly. His forehead was smeared with white stuff. So was Tinu's.

Po stared, bewildered.

"What happens? What happens?" he muttered.

Mana laughed.

"Nar tells us," she said. "He goes to Tinu. He chooses her for his mate. It is his gift to you, Po. A twig breaks. Tinu hears. She is clever, Po. She asks, *Is that Po? Why does he watch?* Nar tells her. She says, *Tinu is not Po's gift. Nar, I do not choose you. Go.* Nar goes. He sends you away. He comes back. He says, *My gift to Po is given. Now, Tinu, I choose you for my mate. It is my choosing. Do you choose me?* Then Tinu says, *Nar, I choose you.*

"Oh, Po, Tinu is happy, happy!"